LAST DAYS OF COLBOSH

Last Days of Colbosh

C. L. Roberts

 iUniverse

LAST DAYS OF COLBOSH

iUniverse books may be ordered through booksellers or by contacting:

iUniverse
1663 Liberty Drive
Bloomington, IN 47403
www.iuniverse.com
844-349-9409

ISBN: 978-1-4401-8892-3 (sc)
ISBN: 978-1-4401-8893-0 (e)

Print information available on the last page.

iUniverse rev. date: 06/18/2024

Acknowledgments

There's a lot of work that goes into writing a book, and I would like to thank those who helped me along the way. I couldn't have done it without their support and guidance. First, my wife Erica and her family; my mother and father for always being there; my grandparents Cleary and Roberts; my aunt and uncle, Anthony and his wife Sarah; Darrel and his family; and Harley boy: he'll never be forgotten by his family and friends.

CHAPTER ONE

(C.E.F) Colonial Earth Force
Deep Space Station 4
Deep space near the Artran border

Admiral Eugene Miguel Frost stood by the coffee pot in his quarters onboard his ship the *Dauntless,* wondering if he had done the right thing by ordering the extermination of an entire race? Was the price worth it? If the Command Council was to put him on trial today, then the answer would be an unequivocal yes. Many of those fat and tired bastards remembered the last war they had with the Artrans. In all honesty Frost should be applauded for his actions. No one must know, though; only he would endure the burden of his actions. Perhaps one day the truth of his actions would be known, and by then it would be up to the history writers to either mark him a villain or the savior of the human race.

The last few drops dripped into the glass container. He poured himself a cup, added sugar, stirred it with a spoon, and then walked over to the parasteel window near the kitchen counter. Outside his flagship the *Dauntless,* the newest ship of the fleet, the C.E.F. *Dawson* was undocking from one of the many multi-limbed berths located around the space station's exterior.

God, it was a beautiful ship! The lines arched back in seamless perfection. No weapon ports were visible; they were safely tucked away beneath the new armored hulling, allowing the ship to take far more damage than the existing ships. The engines were twice as large, allowing it to outmaneuver any ship in his fleet. Several times Frost had been tempted to move his flag to the *Dawson*, but the *Dauntless* had been home for so long now, he couldn't dream of ever leaving her behind. It had been his ship, ever since the war with the Artran. It had survived with him then, God only knew how, and it would continue to do so if he had anything to do about it.

At least there was peace with the Artran Council for now. A peace he intended to keep at all costs. Humanity couldn't afford another conflict of the magnitude it had endured during that war. Earth itself was still recovering from the devastation. Millions had lost their lives in that conflict, including his family.

He caught a glimpse of a blue light blinking from a reflection in the window over near the couch. He didn't remember turning off the audible alarm for the communication table.

How long had it been blinking? He stepped up to the table, which was near his long L-shaped couch, sat his coffee down on the communication table, and clasped his hands behind his back.

"Open communication," he said, straightening out his back.

A stream of blue light appeared above the table, collecting into the shape of a broad-shouldered man dressed in a commander's jacket. Julius was the commander of the station and he was young, almost as young as Frost had been when he had taken command of the *Dauntless*. That was almost a decade ago, but that was neither here nor now. The commander stood at attention with a very machine-like rigidity, as if he had a steel pipe for a spine. His uniform was nicely pressed and his face cleanly shaven.

The commander, in Frost's opinion, had been molded by the Greek sculptors, with high cheekbones and a narrow nose.

"Commander?" he said.

"We've picked up a distress beacon from the *Georgia*, sir."

"And the other ships that were with her?"

"Nothing, not since we lost contact with them."

"And the colony?"

"Still nothing. It's as quiet as when we sent the fleet to investigate it."

"Very well, Commander. Prepare our fleet to move. We're going to investigate this distress beacon."

"If I may speak freely, sir?"

"Of course, Commander. You know you always have my ear."

"This feels like a trap. Whatever is attacking us on our borders is methodical. It stays one step ahead of us every time."

"I understand your concern. Whatever it is that's laying a trap for us, I intend to walk into it fully prepared."

"Sir?"

"Ambassador Lor'ta has assured me that the Artran Council will be sending us additional support to discover this threat and put an end to it."

"That's excellent news, sir."

"Go now and prepare the fleet."

He saluted the commander and had half turned toward his window when he noticed that the commander had not ended the communication yet. The commander's figure was still standing frozen with his hands down by his sides and his eyes locked just above his head.

"Was there something else?"

"Begging your pardon, sir, there is."

"Go ahead?"

"We've recently received a report of a surviving Rackturn Nomad by the name of Colbosh on the planet Septis Four."

Frost paused for a minute and rubbed his chin with his thumb and forefinger. If he remembered right a scientist named Rackturn was the one that discovered a roaming race of aliens; and they were named after him, not that they didn't have a name for themselves. No one could understand a word they said until a translation matrix was developed. No one ever referred to them as Rackturns though, just Nomads. The name of the planet also sounded familiar to him, but why? He couldn't remember.

"Grant," he said. "I sent her there."

"About a week ago."

"Do we know what the Nomad is doing there?" And would this survivor jeopardize his relations with the Artran?

"As far as our information tells us, he was hired by the Grey Stone Mining Corporation. Beyond that we have no more information. More than likely they are hiring up thugs to help keep the workers in line. After all, the majority of citizens there are prisoners."

"Get me a communication to Septis Four. I wish to speak to Commander Grant."

His eyes were already wandering away toward the bedroom door as Julius saluted once more and the blue hologram flickered out. In his mind's eye, he could see Grant standing in the doorway with nothing on but a nightgown, her long red hair flowing down past her shoulders. She was turning away from him, walking toward the bed as she untied her robe's belt and let the whole garment slip down from her body.

As his eyes continued to drink her in, he caught sight of the large yellow stain on his white carpeted floor. The dream was over. Grant no longer stood by the bed. All he saw now was the big ugly spot left by her dog. He had called in several cleaners, but none of them could remove the stain. The only solution had been to order new carpet from Earth, but being this far out, it would take a month before he would receive it.

The blue light was flickering off the wall near the bedroom door. Frost peeked into the bedroom once more, just to see if Grant was there in bed waiting for him. In his mind he already knew the answer, but he had to confirm it to himself, in case there was a chance.

He took in a deep breath, held it for a second with his eyes closed, and exhaled slowly before he spoke. "Open communication."

As usual when she was on duty, Grant's hair was tied back in a thick knot. Her uniform was neatly pressed, but there were dark bags under her eyes.

"Admiral," Grant said with a salute.

He could see her lips pressed tightly together. He guessed that she was probably grinding her teeth as she had done on several occasions when she had been mad at him. "How are you doing, Commander?" he said.

"Is the admiral asking a personal question, sir?" Grant asked, locking eyes with his.

"You know damn well what I mean, Grant!"

"If you call waking up every morning with sand in your hair good, then I'm great, sir. Thanks for asking. Now what is it that you really want, Admiral?"

"Continue with this tone, Commander, and I will have you up for court martial."

Her hands left her sides and crossed over her chest. She glanced away from him for a moment and she blew out a deep breath before her arms returned to her sides.

"I have received news that a surviving Nomad by the name of Colbosh was recently hired by the mining company," Frost told her.

Grant did not speak right away. Her eyes continued to gaze down into his until she turned away for a couple of seconds. He figured she was consulting with someone nearby, but he could not hear what was being said.

"We do have a record from the company about Colbosh. It appears he was hired about two weeks ago. Is there a connection between this Colbosh and what happened on his planet, Admiral?"

"That information is confidential, Commander," he said. "I want you to detain this Colbosh, Commander. He is not to be questioned until my retrieval squad arrives."

"Detaining Colbosh may be a problem, Admiral," Grant said. "It appears that Colbosh left the protection of the city walls several days ago and has not been heard from since. The company has pretty much given him up for dead."

He clasped his hands behind his back again.

"Admiral? Is there anything else you need?"

"Keep an alert out, Commander, just in case this Nomad Colbosh isn't dead yet."

"Understood, sir," Grant said, throwing a salute up.

He returned the salute and walked back to the parasteel window, twisting his wrist around in his grasp as he looked out at the *Dawson* moving into formation next to the C.E.F. *Africa*. The *Africa* was an older ship, about half the size of the *Dawson* and with half the firepower. Most of her armaments were bristling from the sides and front of the *Africa*. There were no graceful lines like the *Dawson* exhibited.

Why was this Colbosh on Septis Four? He thought. Was he there because of the other alien, the Qui'than Frost had sent there, or was it just coincidence? Regardless, if Colbosh was dead then there was nothing to worry about. Besides, it was unlikely the ambassador even knew about the survivor yet. Still, this one survivor could undermine everything.

He turned back to the communication table. "Commander Julius," he said.

The light on the table blinked red at first. Several seconds later the light turned blue and an image of the commander appeared above the table again.

"Admiral?"

"I want you to pull any records we have of this Nomad. If he was living on Chevron Five, then he probably served in the human military."

"I've already pulled the files. It appears our Nomad did serve us during the war. From beginning to end, Admiral, he received several awards, including a Star Cluster."

"That's very impressive, Commander. Do we have any images of this Nomad?"

"Yes sir. Sending you one now."

The image of the Commander vanished from the table and the image of the Nomad replaced it. Its reptilian face was the same as other Nomads, with a large snout that stuck out and large pointed teeth in its mouth. The eyes were set straight ahead, like a human's, but there was no color differentiation, just solid black orbs. The odd thing about this Nomad was its skin color; it was a shade of greenish blue that was out of the ordinary. All the Nomads Frost had served with were almost gray or darker green in appearance. The bony ridges on the head and neck were the same.

"Do you think this Nomad has information about what happened on his world?" Julius said.

"No, Commander, I think he's just a lucky survivor."

A survivor that might cost Frost everything he had built with the Artran. *For your sake, Colbosh, let's hope you're already dead,* he thought.

CHAPTER TWO

Grey Stone Mining Corporation
Septis Four, outside of Novick City

The only sound Colbosh could hear was the wind, followed by gusts of sand blasting into his covered face. The only color he could see was a dull gray as the sun faded in the nonexistent distance. One foot here might as well be a mile in distance. A single degree off in direction and you could wonder the dunes for eternity. He had brought along a direction finder that was built into a unit that he wore around his gloved wrists, but it had stopped functioning several hours ago. His only hope at finding his way back to the safety of the city was to follow a herd of Bomars that were following the scent he had laid out several days ago. He had been hired by the mining company to eradicate these creatures from the nearby city, but instead he had been using them to his own means. Except now he was at their mercy. He should have gone back to the city hours ago instead of venturing out furtherer to find out how many of the beasts had picked up the scent.

He couldn't see them so much as he could smell them. It was a sour weed smell. They were close by; he couldn't see them yet, but that was a good thing.

Bomars were extremely carnivorous; they fed off the Gomas that burrowed beneath the sand. If he got too close to them, it was possible they would pick up vibrations from his movements. Their eyesight was bad but they had special pads beneath their feet that allowed them to pick up vibrations beneath.

He stopped at the crest of a dune. Several meters away he could make out the outline of several Bomars. They stood on four legs, had torsos covered with long hair that extended out into long necks. Their heads were large, with big teeth protruding from a maw that could swallow several large boulders. There were no visible eyes, just a white ridge of some kind where eyes should have been which stretched across their faces. From Colbosh's knowledge of the creatures, the ridge was geared toward smell.

One of the Bomars looked back in his direction. He froze in place. It made a loud noise with its head tilted back. The noise bellowed over the wind and then it looked back in his direction once again.

The weapon he carried on him was powerful enough to drop maybe one or two of the creatures before they reached him, but after that the rest of the herd would zero in on his scent or the vibrations of the weapon and he would be no more. His quest for vengeance would be over. The death of his people would no longer have meaning and those responsible would never be found. This was not how it should end.

Another Bomar looked in Colbosh's direction. His hands were already digging beneath his cloak for the weapon he had strapped behind his back. If they started coming in his direction, he would take the time to try and take head shots. It was possible that with a couple of good shots he could take down several before they were on top of him.

The two Bomars looking in his direction were joined by a third and then a fourth. The weapon was in his grasp and drawn out from beneath his cloak. He went down on one knee, ratcheting the round chamber back. The AR- 517 was an excellent human weapon. It had a tactical scope on top designed for desert warfare. He flipped the lid cover back off the scope and put his goggled eye to it. A colored display filtered out most of the blowing sand and he was able to line up the crosshairs on one of the heads of a Bomar. The scope factored in wind and distance for the shot. If he shot now, the Bomar he had lined up in the sights would go down. There was no doubt about that.

His finger relaxed on the trigger and he pressed the safety release. In the distance one of the Bomars bellowed again. Through the scope he could see the creature move. It was scratching one of its large legs into the sand. Then another joined in. Soon all four were digging their feet in the sand with vigor. The Bomar in Colbosh's scope stuck its mouth down into the hole made by their feet. When it lifted its head out, a baby Goma was wiggling in its maw. The Goma was only about half the size of the Bomar.

Black blood squirted from the Goma as the beast bit down hard into its long tubular body. A meaty part of the Goma fell away and the three other beasts dove for it with their long necks. He didn't watch the rest; instead he stood back up and pressed the weapon's safety back in place. It took several minutes for the beasts to devour the Goma, and when they were done they began to fall away one by one, back on track to the city. .

Dim, whose name derived from his function as a "droid interpreter matrix," floated high up in the ceiling of Novick City. There were several large structural beams surrounding him; he was the size of an adult human head with a few lenses that protruded from its armored shelling and was easily small enough to fit between two support beams laced together. From here he could not be seen by anyone but he had an excellent view of almost everything. For the past couple of days he had remained here cracking into the local security channels. Twenty-one hours ago he had succeeded. He now had a direct link with city security and all military channels. About an hour ago, an arrest warrant had been issued for his owner Colbosh by Commander Grant.

There was no indication on any channel that his owner had arrived back in the city. Most of the communications for the past several days had indicated that his owner was dead. The mental link he shared with his owner was silent, but that had been anticipated due to the thick walls of the city and the distance his owner was traveling away from him. This did not mean his owner was dead as some had conjectured.

In fact his owner had been due to arrive at the east wall door about an hour ago, according to Dim's internal database. Due to the nature of his owner's mission, his database was full of examples of his owner being behind schedule. Every hour his owner was overdue, though, the odds went up that his owner had met his fate in some way without Dim's knowledge.

Without his owner, what would he be? There was no such thing as freedom in his programming. If his owner didn't show up within the next day or so, he would be required to go and find his body.

"Security Team Alpha!" A male voice broke in over the military channel. "Someone has just tried to access the east side door, please investigate immediately!"

"On the move," another voice said.

Dim was also on the move. It had to be his owner. He was the only alien that had been reported outside the city and he had been given a security card that would have allowed him access in or out of the city wall. The rest of the population was prisoners and their movements were extremely limited.

Two military guards in full armor were already standing by the door when Dim arrived. One was standing by the door near the control panel, while the other stood back with his weapon lifted into firing position. Dim's link with his owner was still not working; he couldn't warn him that he was now wanted. If he intercepted the guards, though, it might give his owner an edge over them.

"Greetings, Masters," he said, floating near the guard.

The guard turned his weapon on him. "Hold it right there, droid! What's your purpose here?"

"Masters, I am a Droid Interpreter Matrix," he said.

"What's your purpose?" said the guard with the gun aimed at him. The guard by the door also had his weapon trained on Dim now.

"I provide dialectic interpretations for my owner."

"And where is your owner?"

There was a strong banging noise from the door.

"I believe my owner is behind that door."

"Who is your owner?"

"My owner's name is Colbosh."

"Okay, droid, stay there. Thomas, scan the droid. Let's make sure he's not carrying anything."

There was another loud bang at the door as the other guard left and approached Dim. He moved a small scanning device in his hands side-to-side and then stuck it back in a pouch on his belt.

"It's clean, sir."

Over the security channels Dim heard the guard with the weapon still drawn on him asked to report to Commander Grant. The commander was giving the guard permission to open the door. Dim and his owner were to be taken to the local security cell to wait for questioning. Grant had also routed more troops to this position.

Two more guards arrived within sixty-eight seconds. They took up positions around the door in a fan pattern. Then they opened the door. A swirl of sand blasted in, darkening Dim's visual receptors. The link with his owner was instantly restored. He poured the information to him about their immediate capture, but it was too late; the sound of gunfire erupted around him.

Colbosh could make out the outline of the large wall of Novick City. From this distance it looked like a small mountain rising out of the sand. He could no longer see the Bomars but their scent was still heavy in the air. They had moved to the south of him for now. Perhaps they had picked up the vibrations of some more Gomas in the area, he thought. He no longer needed them; soon he would be in the city and he could finish his task there. He hoped that the beasts would make their way back toward the city in time to give him the diversion he needed.

He told himself not to worry about it. Once the beasts got close enough to the city, they would pick up the vibrations from the machinery and mining going on. They would be on the city wall just as they had in the past from the records his droid had found for him. When the company first arrived here, the beasts had destroyed their first mining facility, killing all of the workers. Since the construction of the walls, the beasts had been kept out, but it didn't stop them from attacking from time to time. The company had taken precautions to help lure any Bomar herds from getting too close. The creatures were a lot smarter than the company thought, however. So the company was forced to try and eradicate the creatures before they got close. This was what Colbosh had been hired for.

At the edge of the wall, he found the light for the outside door blinking red just above a pile of sand almost covering it up. He dug into the sand, slinging it to the sides until he uncovered enough of the door to insert his key card in the control panel. On the first attempt it stayed red, so he yanked it back out and forced it back in. This time the light over the control panel turned green. The outer door opened by rolling out of the way, revealing a small alleyway from the outside door to another door at the far end.

Somewhere behind him he heard the howl of a Bomar. They must have found what they were after and now they were moving back in his direction again. This was excellent; his plan was falling into place. Soon he would have one of the convicts that had been responsible for the destruction of his world and he would get the answers to his questions, regardless of who he had to kill.

After a few steps into the alleyway the door began to roll back into place behind him. There was a small light illuminating the alleyway. Sand was up to his ankles as he stomped to a stop in front of the second door. The key card was still in his gloved hand. He forced it into the slot on the control panel and the light stayed red. The second time he tried it, the light remained the same. It was after the third time he realized something was not right. He tried to feel for the link with his droid, but there still was no little hum in the back of his mind where the droid's voice used to be.

There was something in the construction of the wall that was blocking his signal. It had to have been the new metal Grey Stone was extracting from this place. The company had obtained a very lucrative contract with the military to use this new metal in the construction of its newest ships.

If his access had been cut, then that meant military soldiers were on their way to bring him in. He didn't have much time to act. This alleyway was a terrible place to be caught in a gunfight. He had no room to move. Now that he was inside, he doubted that he could get back out.

He left the key card in the control panel and dug into his cloak. His fingers found the package wrapped up inside his inner pockets. After he pulled it out, he pulled the plastic wrapping off it. The material was sticky on his gloves and it almost took his glove with it as he slapped it to the inner door. There was a small plastic box attached to the substance and he pressed a button on the box. A yellow light lit up and he stomped through the sand back up the alleyway. His AR-517 was in his left hand, lowered down at his side. With his right hand, he smashed his gloved fist into the light in the alleyway, putting it into total darkness.

He took a kneeling position down at the far end of the alleyway. He flipped the lens off his scope and peered down it again. The scope was now displaying the alleyway as if it was completely lit. With his other hand, he felt along the side of the weapon until he found the small depression built into it. He would wait until the door started to open, then he would press the button. If the guards were dumb enough, they would be close to the doorway and hopefully his weapon would take out a majority of them.

If they had some intelligent soldiers here then they would be fanned out away from the door. The explosion still might take one or two of them out, but there might be more to deal with.

He heard the grind of the door before he saw it start to roll out of the way. There was a buzz in the back of his head and then he heard Dim's voice talking to him. Dim was warning him about something, but his eye had focused on his first target as the door continued to roll out of the way. The crosshairs were lined up on the soldier's neck. It was a small target, but it was the only exposed vital spot. He pulled the trigger.

Blood spraying from the soldier's neck was the last he saw before he placed the crosshairs on another guard. He pressed the button on the side of his weapon. The force of the blast knocked him backwards, but he remained in control of his weapon. On his belly, he repositioned himself to fire his weapon again.

Through the scope he placed the crosshairs on a young human with his helmet half off. The young man had blood streaming from his ears and his mouth hung open. The human turned his head toward Colbosh, his blue eyes wide. Colbosh pulled the trigger.

He could see no more movement; he pushed himself to his feet and approached the end of the tunnel. How many dead, he thought. With the link now working between him and his droid, he would be able to find out how many of the troops survived the blast and what their current positions were.

"Owner!" The response came back in his head as dialogue. "Three of the troopers are down. The fourth is taking a position several feet to the left of the entrance. Display coming up now."

In Colbosh's mind he could see a thermal image of the trooper, standing just where his droid had told him.

"The trooper is preparing a grenade, Owner."

The visual displayed in front of him like a small projection showed the trooper reach for something on his belt, pull it loose, and step away from the wall. There was little time to react. He took off at a dead run the rest of the way to the end of the tunnel and threw himself out the end as an explosion erupted behind him. He tucked into a roll, and when he came to a stop with one knee up he was already bringing his weapon to bear on the lone remaining trooper.

A gush of air exhaled from his covered mouth as something hit him in the chest. His right hand had loosened around the grip of his weapon and he almost lost it. Around him he could hear bullets hitting the ground. He forced his weapon to his shoulder and without scope-aided aim, he pressed the trigger in rapid succession.

Some of his bullets hit the trooper in the armor. The trooper stumbled back for a second, which gave him the time to bring the scope to his goggles and fire.

"Owner!" Dim said. "More troopers have been diverted to this location. I fear that someone has uncovered our true purpose here. Should I begin planning our escape route?"

"Where is the Qui'than?"

"We do not have much time, Owner," Dim said.

"The *Qui'-than!*" He growled and tossed the head wrapping to the side. Now his face was totally uncovered. He could see the area around him much better. Blood from the dead troopers was pooling on the sandy floor. There was no movement from their bodies; they had come to rest like so many of the aliens he had killed in the past, to rest in bent-up or twisted postures. Some had their legs and hips turned opposite from their torsos; others had curled up into a ball on the flooring. It was always the same, just like the smell.

It was a putrid decay smell, like someone had just dug up an old patch of earth. He would remember these troopers' faces, not that his memory was that great, but his link with his droid provided instant access to any combat he had been involved in. Dim would give him a full breakdown about whom he killed, what their rank was, and so on.   He could never forget what he had done, not that he cared to. The troopers that fell today were the first on a long list of victims that would lead him to discovering who had killed his people.

"Owner, the Qui'than is in the local club, second floor. There is another person with him. A human female."

"Show map," Colbosh said. The visual in front of him changed to an over-view of the city. His droid had highlighted in red a direct path to the club, and he also displayed the current position of the troopers heading in their direction. There were at least twenty yellow dots and they were coming in packs of five, each group taking different routes. He might have five minutes at most before they intercepted them.

The club was toward the center of the map and the troopers had already passed it. He was situated at the east wall near the sewer plant. Further to the north was the command center, trooper housing. To the west were the mining facilities and prisoner quarters.

If he and Dim made their way into the sewage plant, they could keep the trooper forces divided up. The odds were still against him.

He took off at a jog in the direction of the sewer plant, and Dim changed the red marking from the club to the plant. An estimated calculation was displayed for him at his present speed to his arrival there. A secondary calculation told him the possible interception time of the other troopers.

The troopers were still about two minutes behind him when they reached the gated fence. He shot the lock loose from the fence and took off at a run. The visual in front of him showed one group of the troopers closing in behind. There was a small series of steps in front of him that lead to a metal door. He slammed into it with his full weight and it broke from its hinges. The impact made him off balance and he rolled past the door onto a metal grating.

From behind he heard bullets rip into the opening. When he looked at the visual, he could see the troopers closing in on the door. They were fanning out. Behind that group another set of troopers was moving in through the fence. The grating ahead of him was a catwalk over several pits of chemicals. The place reeked of human scum. Humans were about the foulest smelling creatures in the galaxy.

"Owner, I have identified an escape route for us."

Colbosh was watching the grating below his feet. The greenish chemicals below him bubbled up as he dashed toward the other end, where there was another door and a series of steps off to the side that led down to the chemical vats. The display Dim had been sending him changed from the blue dots that represented the troopers to an interior map of the sewage plant. There was a route highlighted in yellow through the door ahead, along with something circled in red in the same room he was in now.

"There is a chlorine reservoir several meters to our left. I will plant an explosive there while you hold the troops by the other door. In the other room is a service tunnel that leads beneath the city."

Despite the foul stench around him, Colbosh smelled the repugnant odor of humans entering the building. He had made it to the other door at the far end of the catwalk when he spun around with his weapon raised, laying down a barrage of fire to the other end. The door was already partially open as he backed into it. His droid had already dropped low and was heading for the chemical reservoir. The only job he had now was to hold the humans at bay long enough for Dim to achieve his mission.

The bullet count was down to six, and then he would have to ditch the weapon for his backup pistol. The troopers had been doing a good job so far keeping him confined behind the door frame while they made their way down the catwalk. His droid was still providing him information from the display of the interior map of the sewage plant. The other set of troopers were entering in through the other side of the building. Soon he would be trapped.

"Accomplished!" he heard Dim announce in the back of his head. There was a pause long enough in the firefight to let him line up a shot. A trooper marching up the catwalk was replacing a clip in his weapon when Colbosh's bullet ripped through his neck.

He was down to five now and there were four troopers still coming toward him. The troops approaching him from behind were getting closer; he could smell them now. Some tried to mask their scents with chemicals, but that only made them smell worse.

"I need cover now!" Dim said.

Despite the hail of bullets pounding the door, Colbosh twisted the gun around the edge of the door frame and let loose a last blast of fire. When the gun clicked empty, he dropped it onto the flooring and pulled the .40-caliber pistol from beneath his cloak and continued firing. His droid floated up from the flooring, but took several hits which ricocheted off its armored hulling before floating past him.

The nine shots Colbosh had in his pistol were down to three when he was able to shut the door behind him. He took his empty AR-517 and jammed it in the door handle. It wouldn't stop them for long, but it would buy him some time.

From around a metal tube below him, a bullet hit him in the shoulder. His body armor absorbed most of the impact, but it still hurt. There was no time for pain, only reaction. The catwalk he was on made him a visible target to the troopers. He had to get off here and quick. His droid took several more direct hits as it dropped down toward the floor. Colbosh followed suit, dropping to his knees and rolling off the side. Bullets echoed around him and another impacted his chest armor.

His feet were the first to hit the ground and his knees absorbed the rest of the impact. Dim was nearby, low to the ground with all visible lights turned off. It was easy for the droid to blend in with the rest of the piping and machinery in the room.

From the visual Dim was sending him, Colbosh could see the exit route highlighted on the map. At a dead run he would be able to pass by any of the troopers in the room.

There was an explosion in the other room that rocked the foundation. Fire erupted from the catwalk along with a human ablaze. Now was the time to act. A full sprint made his lungs hurt as he inhaled the noxious fumes. Dim followed behind him. The access door had an old-style turn-wheel handle on it. It didn't take much force to turn it. Once the door was open there was a stairway leading down into an unlit tunnel.

On the display Dim was sending, the troopers had abandoned the building. None had followed them into the access tunnel. Soon they would be at the club and he would learn what info he needed.

"Owner! There are reports that a herd of Bomar has been sighted near the wall. Commander Grant is diverting some of the task force hunting us to the outer wall. Your diversion is working!"

Would it divert them enough, though? The creatures were a huge threat to the city, but only if they attacked. The mating scent he had used to lure them here should have been a strong motivator for them.

"Troops have begun searching the access tunnel, Owner. Commander Grant has also turned off the Transponder IDs. I no longer have access to the troops' movements. Do we proceed with our mission?"

"No!" he said. It had taken him weeks to learn that the Qui'than that had come to his world on that fateful day was here, and he was not going to stop. The blood of his people called to him, and there would be no rest until the guilty parties had been brought to justice. He would kill every last human he had to, to get the information he wanted.

They didn't encounter any more troops until they exited out of the access tunnel and arrived at the club. There was a line of humans dressed in bright yellow jumpsuits by the door of the club. A lone trooper was checking over the humans before letting them in.

"The Bomars are approaching the wall," Dim told Colbosh. "Grant has ordered all troops to open fire."

He couldn't hear any of the gunfight going on around them, but unless the humans managed to kill all the creatures before they reached the wall, then he still might have time. He had to hurry.

"I will provide distraction, Owner," Dim said, floating away from him toward the line of humans.

Colbosh made his way around toward the back of the line, where a couple of humans of varying colors were huddled together. They were passing a cup of some kind between them. The smell from the cup was toxic; it was a homemade poison humans had made during the war. He had tasted it once and it made him vomit it back up. That had been the last time any human had offered some to him. How they could stand it, he didn't know.

A bearded white man with missing teeth looked down at him. He was almost eye-to-eye with the man, but he was at least a few inches taller.

"Where the hell did you come from?"

There was no time for conversation, so he hit the man in the side of the head with his pistol. The man's eyes were frozen in place as he fell to the ground. The other two men looked as if they were going to protest, but seeing the weapon in his hand, they took off at a run.

Ahead of him he made out Dim locked in conversation with the trooper, so he pushed his way through the line. The trooper didn't notice him until he was almost on top of him, obvious poor training on the trooper's part.

The trooper's mouth parted as Colbosh grabbed him from the side by his shoulder and forced him into his bent knee. With the trooper gasping for air, Colbosh ripped his helmet off and smashed the butt of his pistol to the back of the man's head.

The humans that had been in line dispersed around him in a hurry. Some ran into the club, others disappeared into the city. He took a moment to take the weapons from the trooper. The trooper had been carrying an unmodified AR-517 with one extra clip, and a service pistol. The pistol he placed beneath his cloak, the AR-517 he checked over. He pulled the cartridge out and found a full load, then slapped it back in.

"Chatter amongst the troops on the outer wall report at least twenty Bomars," Dim said in the back of his mind.

Where had so many come from? He hadn't come across that many in the past two weeks since he had been here.

"Three have been taken down," Dim Said. "Grant has ordered all available troopers to the outer defense wall."

Things were looking up. With that many creatures, the troops would be tied up for hours trying to eradicate them.

The club was in disarray as Colbosh entered. Humans were fleeing toward the exits. Those that got in his way he pushed or shoved away from him. Dim floated safely above the crowd. So far he had only spotted one trooper in the building. He was standing amongst the crowd trying to bring the people to order. Colbosh crept up behind the trooper, grabbed the man's chin with one clawed hand and the back of his head with the other. With a swift twisting motion, the man's neck snapped in his grasp. The trooper collapsed to the floor and it was time for Colbosh to move again. The target was close.

A Qui'than had a very different odor than humans. Qui'thans had an ugly exterior which excreted a gooey substance to protect them from their planet's harmful radiation rays. It was a plant-like smell, bitter but not repugnant.

Colbosh vaulted two steps at a time until he reached the top. Some more humans passed him by and he pushed one down the stairway. The blood was roaring in his ears; the Qui'than's smell was growing stronger. Through not the first door, but the second door on the left, the pale wrinkled skin of the Qui'than lay sprawled out on a bed. Its flabby arms were above its head and restrained by cuffs to the bed post. The secretion from its body was sticking to the sheets.

Its small black eyes opened wide. At first it pulled against the restraints.

"Who you?" the Qui'than said in broken English.

The arrogance of the guilty? Soon Colbosh would know everything.

"Who you, who you?"

There was another smell in the room: the repugnant smell of a human. A woman with long black hair emerged from the rest room. She was wearing a translucent flesh wrap with orange strips covering her reproductive organs.

Dim floated up beside the Qui'than as the woman approached Colbosh. About a week ago he had made contact with the woman. She was a local prostitute here.

"You're late," she said.

"My owner thanks you for your patience," Dim said in response to his owner's thoughts.

She stuck out her hand, palm upright.

Colbosh pulled a credit chip from beneath his cloak and slapped it into her hand. The Qui'than was still screaming in the bed as she left the room with a smile on her face.

"My owner wishes to know who helped you," Dim said.

"Who you?" the Qui'than said.

It was trying to convince him that it didn't know what he was talking about. He would continue with the questioning. If that failed, he would try another method.

"If you tell my owner who hired you to kill his people, I'm sure he would be willing to let you go," Dim said.

"Nothing, I know nothing," the Qui'than said.

Its dark eyes dashed back and forth from Colbosh to his droid. It was obviously nervous. He just had to keep pressing. Intimidation had always worked for him in the past.

He let out a growl and showed the Qui'than his teeth. It quivered and strained at the restraints, but the bedpost didn't budge.

"It's no use covering for others. If you just tell my owner what he wants to know, he will let you go," Dim said.

"Nothing, nothing, who you?"

Colbosh placed the barrel of AR-517 in the Qui'than's face.

"I know nothing, nothing."

"It could be possible that its memory has been altered?" Dim said in the back of Colbosh's mind.

That was impossible; the Qui'than was lying. He was just trying to protect himself from whoever was responsible. It was time to try another route. Colbosh broke the post from the bed and with one hand lifted the Qui'than and rammed him into the wall.

The wall crumpled in under the impact and the Qui'than collapsed to its knees. With two strides Colbosh grabbed the thing's restraints and began dragging it from the room. When he reached the top of the steps in the now empty club, he tossed him down it.

The Qui'than let out a series of grunts and cries as it rolled to a stop at the bottom. At first it didn't move but then it wriggled around some.

"Owner, reports from the Command Center are reporting a heavy attack on the eastern wall. Grant is recalling some troops to the inside, to start forming a defensive barrier. Our path to the rooftop should be unimpeded."

At the base of the steps Colbosh grabbed the restraints again. The Qui'than didn't resist much this time as he dragged him along the floor.

Their route through the city to the elevator shaft that led to the rooftop went without incident. He did have to knock the Qui'than in the head with his AR-517 at least once. That knocked it out for a short time, until they were riding up the shaft.

The Qui'than moaned once and its gaze moved slowly from Colbosh to look out through the metal grating at the city streets below. To the east Colbosh could see the wall begin to buckle in. There were troops rushing toward the area.

"Owner, the troops are reporting that the Bomars are breaking through the eastern wall."

He gave no response. The only thing that mattered at the moment was the answer to his questions. The Qui'than could defy him as much as he wanted, but very soon it would have to choose between life and death.

The elevator came to a stop at the top. Colbosh opened the grated door and dragged the Qui'than into the small maintenance room. Control panels blinked on the wall. Ahead was a door where Dim was already punching in a key code from a small arm extended from its armored shell. The door lifted open, allowing a blast of cold, sand-filled air to burst in.

Colbosh shielded his eyes at first, and then with the Qui'than in tow, forced his way through the door.

He wished he had kept his goggles, but things had happened so fast.

His leg bumped into something. He had found what he had come up here for. An old hoisting system was attached to the side of the wall. The Qui'than was fighting to break free from him, but with a butt of his head into the Qui'than's, the creature slumped down to the sand-covered flooring.

He could barely make out the alien crumpled at his feet. It didn't take him long to wrap the hoisting chain around the Qui'than's restraints. Once that was done he lifted the alien to its feet and slapped it in the face. Its dark eyes focused on him.

"My owner wishes to know who helped you kill his people," Dim said. "My owner knows that you were part of the team that destroyed his world's atmosphere generator."

"I know nothing. I know nothing."

The monstrous rapidity of the alien's voice annoyed Colbosh. He kicked it from the side of the city wall. He heard it scream over the wind for a few seconds before he hit the stop. Two Bomars were waiting for the Qui'than down below. He could see one of the creatures move toward the kicking Qui'than's body. Another bit one of the alien's feet. He hoisted it back up, lifting it over the wall.

The alien's eyes had taken on an orange tinge. Its body was secreting more of the goo-like substance than before.

"Please tell my owner who helped you," Dim said.

"Nothing, I know nothing."

"If you just tell my owner the information he needs—"

Colbosh tossed the alien away and let him go further down the wall before pressing the stop button on the hoist. The Bomars were still there at the bottom waiting; the alien was screaming and Colbosh just could barely make out the Bomars fighting over the alien's legs. One of them bit the alien's leg off and the other fought to get it from the first beast's mouth.

When he hoisted the alien back up, its eyes were already closed. It had to have been unconscious, but Colbosh was prepared for that. He pulled a syringe from a small pouch in his belt. The neck was the best place for the injection. The alien's eyes jerked open when the needle punctured its neck. Its pupils were now completely orange and its mouth was moving rapidly, as if it was trying to say something.

"I know nothing."

"If you just tell my owner, everything will be okay," Dim said.

"Nothing."

Its body was shaking uncontrollably. Why wasn't it telling him what it knew? Colbosh let it go, and this time he didn't stop the hoist. Down below there were some roaring noises. He didn't look; he should have, but he couldn't quell the questions rolling through his mind.

"Owner, it is possible that the Qui'than's mind has been altered. Their anatomy is very acceptable to human operations."

Could they have intentionally altered its memory? Now what was Colbosh supposed to do? How could he find the information he needed?

"Owner, I think the Qui'than's life has come to an end."

Half of the Qui'than's body had been bitten away. Colbosh hoisted it up as quickly as he could, but there was nothing he could do now. He dropped the body to the floor of the roof and pulled a knife from his belt. With a sawing motion he severed the head from the alien's dead body.

"Your ship is en route to us, Owner," Dim said.

Colbosh could see it just off in the distance. It wasn't a large ship; it had a cabin and a cockpit, but that was about it. It wasn't that he couldn't afford something better, it was the fact that this ship had become home over the years. He had added several modifications to it, some of them illegal. That wasn't important at the moment. What was important was what he should do with the Qui'than now. How could he get the information he needed from the dead? There was a possibility; it wasn't cheap, but there was a way.

CHAPTER THREE

Dim was plugged into his portable recharger built into the cockpit of the ship. His owner showed up as a red glow from his thermal view and his respiration was steady; he was lounged out in the only chair in the cockpit with his legs propped up on the control displays. For the past two days they had been traveling to a human-colonized research world.

An incoming message flashed across the cockpit display. While plugged into the charger Dim had complete access to all of the ship's controls.

A brief logo of a human DNA strand appeared on the display, along with Zi-tac printed in bold through it. The screen flashed blue for a second and then an image of a young blond woman with her hair pulled back came on.

"This is the secretary of Director Lorna, whom am I addressing?"

"I am a Droid Interrupter Matrix, mistress. I speak on my owner's behalf."

"And your owner's name?"

"Colbosh. We had inquired to the director about—"

"Nobody speaks to the director without coming through me, droid."

"I did not try to insult you, mistress."

He could see the woman look down at something. "Tell your owner he has an appointment with Director Lorna in the morning around ten, and don't be late. The director is a very busy person."

"My owner wishes to discuss with the director—"

"There is no negotiating about this droid. Be here tomorrow morning or forget talking to the director at all."

The communication ended with a flash of the Zi-tac logo and then back to a blank screen. His owner's respiration was still slow and steady, and the thermal had not changed from its red glow. There was no need to inform his owner about the current situation. They would be arriving at the Zi-tac world in plenty of time for his owner to negotiate with the director.

Dim turned the internal frequencies of the ship back to the military channels. There had been several mentions of his owner's name over the past two days on it. His owner was wanted by the military now for the incident at the Grey Stone Mining Corporation.

There was a stench of burning sulfur in the air and the taste of cooper in Colbosh's mouth from the blood dripping from it. The lighting of the mines he grew up in was poor, but good enough for him to see the onslaught of blows that came next from the Nomad of the clan Alar.

The Alar clansman struck him twice more in the face before he could get his guard up; the Alar kneed him in the stomach which bent him over retching. Then with a final kick to the face he collapsed to the grey ash-covered surface. Flashes of people moved around him; he wanted to get up, but his body wouldn't respond.

"Colbosh?" A voice said to him.

It took his eyes a moment to focus in on the blurry face of Shanta, the clan leader of Orbo; which was Colbosh's clan from the time of birth. His mother hadn't survived the experiments the humans had done on her before birth and his father had been gunned down by the human troopers trying to get to her. So he was brought up in the care of his clan.

Shantas' face was deeply scarred from many years of hard labor and fighting, and the right pupil was covered over by her lid and sewn shut. The dark cords used were still visible.

"It would've been better if you had died at birth, Colbosh." Shanta said.

"Time after time you've had to prove yourself a worthy member of this clan and failed. You're no longer welcome amongst us Colbosh."

Shanta stood over him as two more of his clansmen joined up beside of her. "Just lay here and die, the humans won't care, they've made their profit off you."

They left him alone, his body so weak and abused he laid there dozing in and out of sleep, until someone picked him up. The face of a grey skinned Alar clansman held him in his arms. He knew the face because of the tattoo markings laced around the eyes. It was Garjan, the son of Alars clan leader Ponta. Garjan was renowned as a fighter; several of the older members of his clan recently fought him and lost. Why had he picked him up? Were they going to torture him some more? Wasn't it enough that he was now without a clan?

"Relax." Garjan said. "I won't let any harm to you.

"Why?" he said with a cough.

"The others think your weak, because you're different than them. I think they're wrong. So I will teach you how to be strong."

"If I fail?"

"Then you will die. Only the strong survive here."

The world around him faded out of existence and he fell.

The crash to the floor had knocked one of his teeth loose. How long ago was that? Colbosh wondered. It took him a second to recognize his surroundings. There was the control console for his ship with all the lights, then his droid, which was disconnecting itself from its charging station and was floating toward him. It must be close to twenty years ago, he thought. Garjan had saved his life that day in the mines and taught him how to fight. He earned his place in the Alar clan and never looked back.

"Are you okay, Owner?"

The droid had not spoken out loud, but Colbosh heard him in his mind.

Lifting himself up with one hand, he used the other to push his droid away.

"My medical scan indicates—"

Colbosh walked into the next room, closing the door behind him. He was in his small cabin. A single-person cot occupied the room; towards the back was a sink, and just past that was another door to the cargo hold.

He went to the sink, plugged it up, and turned it on cold. The water felt good to his mouth. Black blood dripped into the water. With his fingers he pried at the loose tooth. It moved slightly in his fingers, but it was still safely attached.

"Owner, I must speak with you."

He wished he could turn his droid off.

"It is of utmost importance, Owner."

He unplugged the sink.

"Did you do what I requested?"

"Zi-tac would not deal with me directly, Owner. They requested your presence today. They would accept no other offer."

Why did they want him in person? Unless they were going to turn him in, Colbosh thought. After the incident at the mining world, he would be a wanted criminal now. That didn't make sense, though; Zi-tac was out of C.E.F. administration. In essence, they were above the law.

Perhaps they wanted something from him?

"We will be landing in the next ten minutes, Owner."

This had better work, he thought. Justice must be served for his people.

Colbosh watched from the cockpit as the ship descended over the frozen landscape. Zi-tac was a large glasslike structure built into a mountainside. A blizzard was blowing around the structure as they approached a slit in the side of it, lit up with red lights as they flew into it.

Inside the landing bay he saw a couple of ships parked to the left. A platform was stretching out to connect with his ship. Several men dressed in gray armor were entering into the docking bay. Two of the three took positions by the door; a third was approaching his ship.

"Do you think there here to arrest you, Owner?" Dim said.

There was only one way to find out.

He took a black cloak from his cot, touched the panel by the door to the cargo bay, and watched as it descended open. The man he had seen through the display was standing at the ramp with his hands clasped together in front of him. Part of the man's face was a deep patchy red.

"I'm Sergeant Patterson. I'll be your escort to the director's office."

"Is there a reason for this escort?" Dim said.

Colbosh stepped up in front of the sergeant.

"I remember you," Sergeant Patterson said, locking eyes with him. They were dark and emotionless. His droid didn't have a response for him yet; his database should have been able to identify the man by now.

"We were on the *Lexington* together," Patterson said.

"Patterson was a lieutenant at the time, Owner," Dim said in his head. "Patterson won the Star Cluster for leading the charge onboard the Artran ship, after the *Lexington* had been lost."

There had been lots of smoke, and dead bodies, some human, and some of the leather-skinned Artrans with their hairless bodies and cricket-like legs. Colbosh had been a part of the attack.

"I'm sure you remember," Patterson said. "You killed many of the Artrans that day. We were brothers in arms back then."

There was an acidic smell to the sergeant's stench that was out of place with the other humans standing nearby the door. He had been so young when that event had taken place; it was amazing he could remember it. It was before he had been attached to his droid.

"So what happened, brother?" Patterson said.

There was nothing to be said, Colbosh thought. Justice must be served for his people.

"I can understand revenge," Patterson said. "What you did at Grey Stone was treason. If the director didn't want you protected, I would've already gunned you down. You've got no friends here, alien!"

The Sergeant was challenging him. Why had the director thought it necessary to protect him, much less deal with him? Whatever it was, it had to be important to them.

"Have anything to say for yourself, alien?"

"The director is waiting for us," Dim said for him.

Sergeant Patterson stepped up face-to-face with him. They were about the same height; Patterson was maybe an inch or two taller.

"Step out of line, alien, and I'll put you down! I just want you to understand this before we leave this dock. Is my position made clear?"

"Your position is very clear," Dim said.

Patterson stepped away and motioned with his left hand for them to move. The two troopers by the door were both stepping through the doorway into a hallway. He drifted toward them, and Patterson took up step behind them. The droid was keeping pace beside him.

The hallway past the docking area led into a spacious room. They were about three levels up, and he could see over the railing to the next level down and the bottom floor. People in white smocks and plain clothing walked about the place. Some took notice of him with the troopers around him. He was led to a set of stairways and down to the next level. A fountain was set in the center of the second level and it was shooting water up into the air. Some of the humans were sitting around it, eating food or talking to other colleagues. Through the windows all around him, all there was to see was endless snow blowing around.

The two troopers in the lead came to a stop at a series of doors. A big letter Z with a swooping half circle was emblazoned on the glass door.

"This is as far as we go," Patterson said. "Remember what I said, alien."

He would remember, but if the sergeant stood in his way, he would kill him, too, to achieve his objective. It was nothing personal. The sergeant was a warrior like him, but that didn't make them brothers. Not considering that the sergeant was the alien, not him. Humans had such a narrow view of the galaxy; they felt themselves superior to everyone else. The Artran had changed that view for them.

"Greetings, I'm Miss Lorna's secretary," the blond woman at the all-white desk said. Her hair was pulled back and she had a thick line of pink lipstick covering her lips. She didn't smile, though, as she rose to come around the desk.

"Miss Lorna has been expecting you, Colbosh."

"My Owner is most pleased that the director has chosen to talk to him directly," Dim said aloud.

Dim was interrupting events on his own. Personally, Colbosh would have preferred pushing the woman out of the way and finding the director on his own. Not that it would be too hard to find her in this office. There was the main entrance behind him, and there appeared only one other doorway ahead, which probably housed a couple of offices.

"If you'll follow me," the secretary said.

Her left leg turned slight to the left with each step. Her pants hid the features of her legs beneath them. If he had to guess, she had either injured her leg somehow or was born that way. It didn't impede her pace, however.

She slid a key card into a panel by an all-white door and then turned the black handle. Through the door was gray marbled flooring, with dark wood walls stretching seven or eight feet taller than Colbosh. At the far end was a large white desk near a window, looking out into the heart of the blizzard.

He smelled the woman before he saw her. It was a fruity smell he couldn't quite place but it was familiar. Pear, humans had called the fruit a pear. That's what she smelled like. It masked the woman's sour repugnance quite well.

"Director Lorna," the secretary said. "This is Colbosh and his interpreter droid."

The woman stalked closer. She had dark eyes and her dark hair was pulled back behind her head like the secretary's. She wore a black jacket and pants, with red shoes that smacked the marble flooring with each step. When she got close enough, she extended her hand to him.

Other humans had tried to teach him this way, by shaking his hand. He didn't care for the practice, especially not now.

The director lowered her hand. "An alien with a purpose! Please have a seat." She stepped behind the desk and took a seat.

The secretary was already leaving the room when the director spoke again. "I'm sorry that I haven't been able to speak directly to you before now. With the disappearance of the Kalto Colony, I fear we have had to be extra secretive of late."

"What does the loss of a human colony have to do with my owner's request?"

"Your owner is wanted by the C.E.F.," the Director said, placing her palms on the white desk. "With all of the military forces around this area of space, I didn't want your owner captured."

"Our signals could be coded," Dim said.

"Codes can be broken."

"Besides, I have something to offer your owner. Something we wish to be kept secretive." The director interlaced her fingers.

They wanted him for something; that was why they hadn't rejected him out of hand, Colbosh thought.

"My owner is willing to pay cash for the services," Dim said.

"I'm afraid I had our department pull all of your owner's financials reports, and unless your owner is carrying a ton of credit on him, he can't afford what he wants done. Do you realize how many resources I would have to pull to do what he asks?"

"My owner wishes to know what your offer is!"

"Very simple." She took her hands off the desk and sat back in the chair. "I've sent several teams to investigate an archeological site we uncovered in the mountains. The problem is none of them have ever returned."

"If trained men have been sent, why do you think my owner will be able to succeed?" Dim said.

"All you have to do is go to the site, find out, if possible, what happened to the teams I sent there, and report back what you find. If you find anything important, you are to bring it back with you."

"My owner is a trained mercenary, but he is only one person. Why are his chances of success higher than the others?"

She leaned forward on the desk with her hands out in front of her again. "It's a theory that since we've found DNA from his race around the sight, he might succeed."

"And if my owner refuses your offer?" Dim said.

He wouldn't refuse the offer, Colbosh thought. The longer he went without answers to his questions, the colder the trail became.

"Then your owner will not find his answers."

"My owner agrees to your proposal, as long as you go ahead and start retrieving the memories for him."

"Agreed," the Director said, standing up. "I will have an assistant come by your ship in a few minutes to retrieve the head. Also, I will send you all the coordinates to the site."

The secretary opened the door behind them.

"Now, if you'll excuse me, I have other urgent meetings for the day."

Colbosh stood and walked past the secretary, who closed the door behind him. His droid spoke in the back of his head. "Owner, I am concerned about this mission. I have been hacking into the administrative files here and the director has sent three armed investigative teams to uncover what is at this site. None of them reported back afterwards!"

There was no choice in the matter. Besides, why was some of his race's DNA at the site? His people had been a nomadic tribe for millions of years; perhaps some of them had colonized there at some time in the past.

"We could try to find another method, Owner."

"No."

"There is something else I need to inform you about! Michelle is on the planet."

That didn't change anything; Colbosh had a mission to accomplish and there was no time to fool with that particular human female.

Michelle stood at a bar with a glass of orange liquid in her right hand. A human female with green eyes dressed all in black stood beside her, and kept glancing her way from time-to-time, although she was talking to no one but the air. All the people present, mostly scientists, had wireless interfaces with one another. It was most annoying. You could never tell if a person was actually addressing you or if they were lost in their own conversation.

There it was again. The woman with the green eyes had looked directly at her. Michelle saw her from her peripheral vision. Getting hit on by guys was one thing, but it had been awhile since a woman had checked her out. The real question was how she could convey to this bitch that she wasn't interested.

"You're not a scientist!" a man with a patchy beard said.

He was taller than her, not by much, though, maybe a few inches. He smelled rather sour, as if he had been working out for several hours and not taken a shower afterwards. The smell couldn't avert her from his smile, though; he had nice white teeth and pale red lips.

"Why do you think that?"

He took her in from head to toe with his gray eyes.

"The first giveaway is the combat boots. No one around here wears those unless they're employed in the security force! I'm guessing you're a freighter captain."

Michelle took a sip of the orange liquid. It sent a jolt of fire down her throat and into her stomach.

"You have a perceptive eye," she said. "What's your name?"

"Perhaps I should order you another drink first."

"Did you ignore my question? I asked you your name."

She watched him motion at the white-jacketed bartender and order a beer. Then he turned back to her.

"My name is Syler." After he took a sip of the beer that the bartender had placed in front of him, he leaned closer to her.

"I'm not a very well-liked man here."

Michelle looked back toward the woman all in black and she was gone, as well as an older man that had been standing several feet from her.

"So, why is that, Syler?"

She watched his Adam's apple leap up and down as he tilted his head back and chugged more of the beer.

"I'm sorry," he said, slapping the bottle back down on the bar. "Can we start over? It's been quite some time since I've found an interesting woman in this place."

"You worried you've scared me off?"

He shook his shaved head and took another chug of the beer. This time when he slapped it down, it clunked as if it was empty.

"Don't worry," she said. "You've not scared me yet. Besides, I don't even know what it is that you do, and I don't care to know. Let's just enjoy each other's company right now."

There was that smile again, just before he stopped the bartender and ordered another beer.

"Can I get you another?" he said.

"No, two's my limit."

"A woman with a limit, I like that, shows you like to keep control of the situation."

"Always," she said, swallowing the last of the orange liquid.

"What made you decide to be a freighter captain? I find it strange asking you a question without knowing your name. Could you tell it to me?"

"Now you want to know my name," she said, leaning in closer to him. "Perhaps I wish to remain anonymous for the moment."

"Have it your way, Captain, if I can call you that?"

"That will work for now." She smiled.

He brushed her arm with his hand and let it come to rest on her thigh.

"I haven't given you permission to touch me yet," she said, lifting his hand from her thigh.

"Sorry, Captain!" He returned his hand to the fresh bottle of beer. "So how can I get the captain's permission?"

"How about a game of pool?" She glanced back at the empty pool table near the wall.

"I would like that," he said, starting to get up when a man in combat armor placed a hand on his shoulder.

The armored man said, "We've got to talk!" Then he walked toward an empty table behind Michelle. The tag on the man's armored chest plate read "Patterson". The several bars on his shoulder plates indicated he was a sergeant. Why did a sergeant want this man she had been talking to?

"I'm sorry," Syler said, brushing her arm again. "I would really like to talk to you again, perhaps after I'm done."

"That would be fine, Syler." She watched the man take a seat next to Patterson. Then she turned her back to them with her head half cocked toward them.

"You interested in making some money?" Patterson said.

"Love to!" Syler said. "It's only been two months, and the rest of the boys have been getting restless. So what's this job you want done?"

"Have you heard about what happened at Septis Four?"

"Yeah."

"Well, Colbosh is here, Syler. And the bounty on his head is considerable."

"Why would he come here?"

"I don't know the full details, but what is important is that he has gone to the dig site."

"Then he's good as dead. I've lost several of my men to that site, and Director Lorna can threaten me all she wants, but I'm not sending anyone there again."

"The director believes that Colbosh will succeed. Apparently they found traces of his race's DNA around the site."

Syler laughed. "What does Lorna know?"

"Would it hurt to go there anyway? If Colbosh comes out, then he's yours to collect the money on. The only thing I ask for is whatever the alien finds there, if anything. If it can be brought back—that's all Lorna cares about!"

"I'll do as you ask, Sergeant, but I'm not sending any of my men down into those tunnels. Personally, I think the alien won't come out, but if he does, I'll take care of him."

"I knew I could count on you, Syler. I could during the war and even now you're still a man of honor."

Michelle glanced back for a second to see Patterson slip a small black disk into Syler's hand.

"All the codes and clearances you need," Patterson said, standing up. He looked in her direction once then slapped Syler on the back before parading out the open doorway.

So Colbosh was on this rock. Did he know that she was here? Why hadn't he tried to contact her? She had tried to contact him several times after the accident on his world. At first she thought he had died during the accident, but this was proof he was still alive, and apparently in some sort of trouble.

Patterson had said something about Septis Four and Colbosh being responsible for what happened there. She hadn't heard any news about that. It must have been fairly recent.

Syler got up from the table and headed toward the exit. He never once looked back in her direction. His shoulders seemed squarer now and his head held higher.

She needed to find out more; If Colbosh was in trouble, she owed him to try and help him. He had spared her life once, after all.

She left a wad of cash on the bar and jogged off after Syler. When she found him a few seconds later, he was taking the steps down to the next level. The stairway was fairly empty except for one or two scientists with their white shirts on, walking past, lost in conversation.

"Are you in the habit of running away?" she said, stepping up behind him.

He stopped and looked back at her.

"I have someplace to be."

There was coldness to his voice. "No apology, or even a number I can reach you at?" She pushed him against the wall and he didn't even brace himself to stop her.

"Sorry, Captain," he said, now with a smile.

She leaned her face in closer to his and brushed her lips on his. At first he put his hand up on her shoulder to keep her back, but that melted away as she forced herself up against him and fully embraced him.

His hands rubbed all around on her back and she did the same, until her right hand reached the pocket of his jumpsuit. With her left hand she reached down to rub his balls while she reached down into his pocket with her right. The man let out a soft moan as she rubbed. When her other hand touched the object in his pocket, she slipped it out and placed it in the belt line at the small of her back, then backed away.

"Do you want to come to my quarters?" he said, taking in a deep breath.

Two women had stopped at the bottom of the steps and were looking up at them until she saw them, then they walked away.

"Consider that a sampling of the goods." She started walking up the stairway.

"Wait, how can I contact you?"

"I'll be around," she said, reaching the top of the stairs and bumping into something solid that almost made her lose her footing. When she looked up to see what she had run into, she found Patterson looking down into her face. His brow was furrowed and he wrapped his steel grip around her arm.

"You have some explaining to do!" Patterson said with an aroma of garlic striking her in the face.

Colbosh flew his ship over the frozen mountaintops and down into the valleys. The snow was still whipping hard as he sat the ship down in a small valley in a large mountain range. From inside of the cockpit of his ship, he couldn't make out anything from the floodlights. It was a haze of snow outside.

"Owner, I'm worried that your thermal suiting will not be sufficient for this mission. The current temperature reading is negative thirty degrees outside and we have no idea how long you will be exposed."

Colbosh had moved to his chambers and was finishing buckling the straps of his jacket in place.

"Your body cannot withstand more than thirty minutes exposed to these conditions. I suggest we find an alternative to our situation."

There was no going back; with the thermal clothing he was putting on, he felt confident that he could withstand these temperatures far longer than his droid estimated.

He snapped the last of the gloves in place and then began wrapping his face with a thermal scarf that had a visor built in. It was like the one he had used in the desert of Septis Four, with the exception that this one was black.

The AR-517 lay on his bed. The weapon had a built-in heat generator to warm the user's hands and to make sure that the weapon continued to perform properly in combat. That was the one thing he admired about humans: they could make a weapon.

On his back he had a sleeve where he holstered the shotgun; he kept the AR-517 slung around his shoulder so it was always within close reach.

"Owner, I wish you would reconsider."

Colbosh's growl was muffled by the wrappings, and then lowered the hatch. His droid remained silent as he trudged through the knee-deep snow to the mouth of a cave.

Inside the cave, Dim turned on his flood-lighting, built into the rim just below his armored upper half. Colbosh turned on the light attached to his AR-517 and then the illumination built into his clothing. The cavern was rather large with lots of stalactites and water dripping all over the place.

Up ahead he could see what looked like tents and other equipment frozen in place.

"The information provided to us by Director Lorna indicates that this is the archeologist research site, before they found the tunnels up ahead."

His droid led the way through the camp, which looked as if it hadn't been touched in years, to a crack in the wall of the cave. It was narrow at first; he would have to turn sideways to make it through.

"Past this the tunnel widens and stretches for a kilometer and that is all that is known. Your body temperature has fallen four degrees in the last ten minutes, Owner."

He wasn't going to respond to his droid; besides, he felt fine. He wasn't shaking yet and he felt warm. The thermal clothing was doing its job. It was a tight squeeze through the crack in the wall, but when he made it through he found himself in a tubular tunnel. There was something unnatural about it.

There were stalactites growing from the walls and floor of the tunnel, but it seemed to be perfectly circular, as if it had been carved through. There was no scarring on the walls, like a human drill would have left. Instead it was smooth and refined with cracks here and there from which rocks protruded.

"Owner, we are nearing the end of the tunnel. My sensors are picking up nothing from ahead."

The end of the tunnel opened wider on all sides and they came to a wall with pictorial images engraved into it. There was a large opening directly ahead of them, but the darkness beyond absorbed their light. They could see nothing past the blackness.

"These images correspond to images left behind by the Ancient's owner. There are no known interpretations for them, but this site must at least be several millennia old."

The more Colbosh looked into the blackness, the more disoriented he became; he couldn't focus on the images on the wall any longer and his hands were shaking.

Was it the cold? His droid would've told him if his temperature had dropped even more. He had to press on and he stepped into the darkness.

Past the veil he found himself looking at strange bullet-shaped mounds that had been molded from the earth, but that wasn't the only thing. There were human-sized large stone blocks interspaced among the bullet-shaped mounds. Then there were statues and symbols carved into the stone blocks or standing by themselves.

The features on the statues were nothing like he had seen before. They were of a humanoid form but the faces were elongated and smoothed back with no noses and ridged-back heads with no hair. Each of the statues was dressed in regal robes; some even wore crowns upon their heads.

What was this place? Were these statues of Ancients?

"Owner...,." Dim said before all of its lights went dead and it crashed to the ground.

His head was spinning now; he couldn't focus on anything and he dropped to one knee. Then it stopped, the lights came back on, and his droid hovered back up from the ground.

"I can't explain—"

"A Guardian, but yet not a Guardian has returned," a third voice said, somewhere near them.

The AR-517 was already in Colbosh's hands and lined up with the figure standing before them. It looked like one of the statues had come to life, except instead of stone for a body it had flesh, which was tan and stretched tight to its flat face.

What had it meant by "Guardian"?

"Greetings, Master," Dim said. "My owner's name is Colbosh and he wishes to know what you meant by calling him a guardian?"

"Not a Guardian," the Ancient said. "Your DNA has been corrupted by these humans. Who dares to defile the sanctity of this place? These humans were not even heard of in my time. They're an insignificant species at best!"

"Are you an Ancient?" Dim said.

"I am, but not a living one," the Ancient said. "It appears your species has forgotten everything about us, Colbosh. This place is a tomb for all the greatest of what you call the Ancients. I was the last to be buried here. That was during the Third Eclipse Cycle, before the Artrans nearly destroyed this world."

It was known that the Artrans had been around for a very long time, but were they the primary enemy of the Ancients? Colbosh thought. It was impossible.

"I understand your confusion, Colbosh," the Ancient said in his language.

"Where did the Ancients go?" Dim asked.

"Not even I know where the Ancients have gone. When I was buried here, my people were at the height of their power. War had been raging with the Artrans for several decades and we had pushed them back to the far corner of the universe."

The Ancient stepped closer to Colbosh and extended an elongated finger toward him.

"Your race was slaves to the Artrans; we freed you from them. The Artrans bred you like cattle to be warriors for their race, but it worked against them. They put too much free will in your DNA. When your race rose up against the Artrans, it marked the turning stage in the war."

The Ancient lowered its hand back to its side.

"With the help of your people, we crushed the Artrans and banished them to a little world with hardly any resources. It was your job to keep them there,

Colbosh, and your people failed in that task.   They were never meant to come back to power. That is all I know about those days and that is why I referred to you as a Guardian."

None of his people had ever spoken of this task. In fact, most of his people had broken apart into separate tribes a long time ago and fled into space, because they were constantly fighting each other. That had been evident even as a child growing up on one of the human mining worlds. Members of his clan were always targeted by another.

The Ancient's head turned to the side for a moment, looking away from him.

"Owner!" Dim said in the back of his mind. "My sensors have detected some movement from the ceiling above us."

The Ancient looked back at him. "You've brought more humans here!"

"It's as I feared. Your kind has been corrupted. You're not worthy to be considered Guardians anymore!"

Dim said, "Owner, we're being surrounded!"

Michelle sat in a cell looking at the blank white walls with her elbows propped up on her knees and her face resting in the palms of her hands. Where had she gone wrong, she thought. *I was only doing what I thought was right. Now what's going to happen to me?* More importantly, what was happening to Colbosh?

It would be her fault if Syler injured him, and that was something she wasn't prepared to face. Not since Colbosh had saved her life; she owed him something, after all, but what could she do from in here? There was no means to contact anyone and the guards had ignored her ever since her arrival.

There was a clanking noise from the door near her cell. Michelle lowered her hands from her face and sat up some. If it was a guard, maybe she could lure him in here and take him out.

Director Lorna and her secretary stepped through the doorway, followed by Sergeant Patterson.

"Explain to me again," Lorna said, "why Michelle is locked up."

"Director, as I've explained before, she was caught stealing. I had every right to lock her up."

"Let me guess who she stole from. Was it one of your mercs, Sergeant? Don't be surprised about what I know. There's one thing I have learned about being a director, and that's that you can't trust anyone, Sergeant!"

"Director —"

"Silence! I know you sent Syler to kill Colbosh! That's the secret you're trying to keep hidden from me. That's why my freighter captain is locked up in here, isn't it?"

Patterson nodded his head.

"Some truth at last. Let me put it to you this way, Sergeant, if your men kill Colbosh before he accomplishes his task for me, I will make sure you spend the rest of your life digging rocks on a mining world! Now release her and get out of my sight!"

Patterson said nothing; instead he pulled a key card from his pocket and slid it into the panel beside the cell. The bars opened and Patterson left the room.

She was free; perhaps there was still enough time to act. If she could get to her ship, she could send Colbosh a signal of some kind. She stood up.

"I'm sorry, Michelle," Lorna said. "Patterson has become more unstable with age."

"Thank you for rescuing me, Director," she said as she approached the door.

"Before you go, I have some questions that need answers."

"What, about Colbosh?"

"It's already too late either way, Michelle. Colbosh is either dead or alive, and nothing you do can change that now."

She turned back to the door anyway. "I really have to go!"

"Michelle!" Lorna called after her. "Did you know that you have a tracking device in your body? It's attached to your spinal column."

Tracking device? What in the hell was she talking about; Michelle had been through several medical checkups in the last couple of years and no device was ever found. If it was true, then who would have placed it there?

"Do you know who placed it there?"

She turned back to face the director, who was moving to stand in front of her. "No."

"Are you sure?"

"Yes, positive."

Where had it come from?

"What if I told you that the only way we discovered it was because Colbosh's droid interfaced with it when you arrived in the system? Otherwise we never would have known it was there."

Colbosh knew about it; why would he want to keep track of her? What was this all about? She needed to go; Colbosh needed her help.

"I'm sorry, Director, but I must really go!"

The director said nothing else, and Michelle ran hard to the docking bay. She knocked down at least two people in her haste, but time was not on her side. Lorna's words kept echoing in her ears the whole time.

"It's already too late."

Colbosh had his weapon raised to shoulder level. The scope wasn't functioning properly; all he could see through it was static as he tried to scan the walls and ceiling. Meanwhile his droid continued to warn him of a threat although it couldn't even identify its exact location.

That's when he caught sight of something falling from the ceiling. It was pitch black, whatever it was, and it was heading straight toward him. He pulled the trigger on his weapon and felt it vibrate in his hands as the bullets sprayed into the darkness. There was no way to know if he had hit something until whatever he had been firing at hit the ground a foot away from him.

Its skin was pitch black and it crawled on multiple legs like a spider, but it reared back on its legs and he could see arms with pincers attached to the thing's torso.

He fired again, this time at point-blank range. The thing burst apart around him. A couple of its legs and one of the pincers blew clean off its body, but the thing kept coming closer as he moved back, trying to keep his distances. The door into the tunnel wasn't too far away.

"Owner, behind you! Dim said."

Colbosh spun. Another one of the creatures clung to the wall just above the tunnel entrance. His bullets ripped into it and it fell away from the wall without a noise. It scurried off behind some of the mounds when he turned to see what had happened with the other creature that had been behind him. He found it on top of him, spraying some kind of liquid onto his clothing from its round head.

One of the thing's pincers grabbed hold of his weapon and ripped it from his hands. With it legs it pulled his feet from under him.

Whatever it had sprayed on him was making him dizzy. The cave was spinning and his legs and arms weren't reacting as fast as they should be. With his free hand he reached for the shotgun strapped behind his back and pulled it free. The head of the thing was bearing down toward his face when he pushed the barrel to its head and pulled the trigger.

It fell off his body and he tried to stand. He stumbled toward the tunnel exit. Everything was blurry.

"Droid," he called out in his mind.

"More are following us, Owner, and approaching fast!"

He turned his upper body to look back for a minute, which was a mistake. In his dizzy state he nearly fell on his face. If he could just make the crack in the tunnel, perhaps he could slow them down some. From one of the pouches on his belt he pulled a human grenade, removed the pin, and dropped it behind him.

A few seconds later he felt it explode and a piece of shrapnel pierced the back of his leg. He fell for a moment, but picked himself up and kept running. Once he reached the crack, Dim went first and he followed behind.

One of the things started to come in behind him and he blasted it back into the tunnel; another followed. He fired again and it went down. Once he passed through the crack he pulled another grenade and tossed it toward the tunnel.

The explosion echoed all around him; he was already deaf from the previous explosion, but what little hearing that had returned to him was gone again, leaving just an annoying ringing in his ears.

"Owner!" Dim said in the back of his mind. "Armed humans are just outside of the cave."

And it was a good bet they weren't here to help him.

Michelle flew her freighter ship low over the mountains, looking for any sign of Colbosh's ship. Devin, her co-pilot, was sitting next to her looking out the window, as well.

"There," she said, dropping the ship into a nose dive.

Outside the window, past the snow, she could see men firing at things coming from the mouth of the cave.

"What in the hell?" Devin said.

Where was Colbosh? Michelle brought the ship down low, she made out a man in armor with a spider-like creature over top of him.

"What are those things?" Devin said. "What have you gotten us into, Michelle?"

There he was! She could see Dim hovering near him; they were at Colbosh's ship, but those spider things were all over top of it.

"Bring me in low over that ship," she said as she got up from the control chair.

"Where are you going?"

"Just fly me low over that ship!"

She made her way to the cargo bay and lowered the ramp. Snow blew in and the cold air made her shiver, but she held tight to a strap attached to the wall. Devin moved the ship around, and Michelle could see Colbosh a few feet away, blasting away at one of the spider things.

He was running towards her now, but so were several of the spider things. She pulled a pistol from the holster she had strapped on during the trip over.

Before Colbosh reached the ramp, however, a human lifted himself in, his armor torn and part of his face bleeding profusely. When the man looked at her, she could see it was Syler.

"Let's get the hell out of here!" he said.

"No!" she said, shaking her head. Colbosh was almost here.

"Leave him!"

Syler crawled toward her.

Colbosh leapt in behind him with part of his body still hanging off the ramp.

"Move the ship Devin, now!" Michelle said.

Colbosh gripped the grating. He was struggling to pull himself all the way into the ship when one of the spider things leapt onto his back and began crawling into the bay.

Michelle aimed the pistol at the thing, but it was so close to Colbosh. Syler was on his back scrambling away from it. Dim had floated into the bay, but no one was doing anything to help, so she held her breath and took aim.

The first shot hit the thing in the head, but it was still moving. The second shot hit it again in the head and this time it collapsed to the floor, unmoving. Colbosh managed to pull himself the rest of the way into the cargo bay and she closed it before going to him.

He was still on the floor when she hugged him, but he didn't hug back. It was always the same reaction. That cold void he tried to create between them.

"This is the last time I save your life," Michelle said.

Colbosh and Dim entered Director Lorna's office. The director was seated at her desk watching them with her dark eyes.

"Greetings, Director," Dim said

She placed her hands on the desk.

"I have the information you want." She tapped something on her desk and the lights went down. The window behind her changed tint and turned into a giant display.

"The images we gathered from the Qui'than's memory were not easy to retrieve. Whoever wanted this knowledge hidden went to great efforts to conceal it. You have a powerful enemy, Colbosh."

An image pulled up on the display. There was no audio, and all he could see was a man dressed in a maintenance uniform pacing around in a control room.

"From the information we gathered, the images are all from the Qui'than's point of view. He arrived with this man, whose name is Reguilis, at your planet's atmospheric generator three weeks ago. They planted explosives in several key areas and then left. An hour later the plant exploded."

How could they have gotten access to the facility? Colbosh thought. The Qui'than was a no-brainer; many technicians used them when radiation work was needed because that gooey substance they secreted protected them. The man, though, who was he and why did he do it?

"All records regarding the identity of the man have been classified by the military," she said. "The only thing we could find out about the man is that he is on Earth, in prison, awaiting self-termination. The military didn't bother to cover up public records."

Earth. He hated Earth, Colbosh thought.

"I believe that concludes our business deal," Lorna said, turning off the display. The lights came back up.

He stood.

"If you want my advice, don't pursue this. Whoever is responsible has a lot of power on his side."

His people deserved justice. Now all he had to do was find a ship to Earth and then find a way into the prison system. Michelle would be the obvious choice to ask, but he didn't want to involve her any more than he had to. She was too much of a distraction when she was near. An obvious weakness of his human genetic side; one he intended to keep suppressed. What the humans had done to him at birth had made him incapable of procreating with others of his race. He was the only one of his kind and he didn't care to pass it on to another generation.

CHAPTER FOUR

Lower section of New York City, Township Apartments
2:00 A.M.

Colbosh and Dim stood in a hallway of an old Earth habitat building. Colbosh was dressed in an old black trench coat that came down to his knees, and a black hat that covered his face well when he tilted his head down. Several tenants were peering at them from cracked doors nearby, and a mixture of smells flooded his senses, the main one being the urine smell emanating from the door outside which they now stood. The white paint was flaking off the wood and the letter B was missing beside the number four. The outline of the B was still there, though.

The travel to Earth had taken awhile and his time was growing short. The man they sought, Reguilis, was due for execution within the hour. Along the voyage, Michelle had found a contact on Earth who could possibly help Colbosh break into the prison system. The man referred to himself only as Joe and gave them instructions to meet him at this address when they arrived.

Colbosh knocked on the door and it creaked open. The urine smell intensified and he saw a man standing by a boarded-up window turn toward him.

"I'm Joe," the man said, tugging at the small patch of white hair growing beneath his lip.

Joe was tall and straight, his skin was pale, and even his blue eyes were pale in color. Joe had no hair to speak of and he looked as if he would break in half if Colbosh struck him.

"Before we get started...," Joe said, stepping over to a medical table situated in the center of the room.

There were several syringes and mechanical devices on a tray next to the table, including dry red bloodstains, which could have come only from a human. What exactly did this man do? Michelle knew him only because he helped her delete her criminal file from Earth's security system. She said he could get Colbosh access to just about anything, but at what cost? The man wanted money; that was obvious.

He pulled a small bag from a pocket in his cloak and tossed it into Joe's hands. Joe opened it and poured the contents onto a small table set up by the boarded window and counted through it.

"This is not the amount we agreed to," Joe said, scooping the blue chips back into the bag and pulling the drawstring taut.

"My owner is only willing to pay you half now," Dim said.

"I want all of it up front or no deal!" Joe said.

"I'm sorry, but my owner will not pay until after you have provided your service to him."

"Then I'm afraid there's nothing I can do for you, alien!" Joe stepped toward the door. "Michelle said that I could trust you, but I can't trust anyone. If they're not willing to pay, then I'm not willing to work."

"Owner, we are running out of time," Dim said in the back of Colbosh's mind.

He didn't have to respond to that; he knew he was running out of time. If Reguilis died before Colbosh got the information he needed, then everything so far would have been wasted. He could be searching for years until he found the rest of the guilty party.

He took another pouch from inside his cloak and tossed it to Joe by the door. Joe almost dropped it, but once he had it secure in his hands, he went back over to the table and counted it out.

"If you would lie down on my table there, we'll get this show going," Joe said, after pocketing the bag.

Joe lifted a case onto the small table by the window and opened it. A greenish light reflected off the wall from the case and Joe stepped over to him, picking up a syringe from the tray.

Colbosh grabbed Joe's arm before he could even get close to his neck. The human was out of his mind if he thought Colbosh would allow him to inject him with something unknown.

"My owner wishes for me to analyze the substance before you inject him with it," Dim said.

"Your owner is wasting time, droid. It's just a light sedative. It will make it easier for him to transition into the prison system."

"It is a light sedative, Owner."

"Now if you would please not interfere with me again," Joe said, "there is much work to be done."

There was a burning sensation in Colbosh's neck after Joe injected the needle, but it dissipated in no time and he was left feeling light-headed. Joe placed pads with wires attached to them to his head and body, and the light directly above him grew so bright and large that he had to close his eyes.

Michelle stood with her fist held high and ready to strike at a bag she had hung in the cargo bay of her ship. She had yellow gloves on that were cracking and peeling in places, letting some of the padding show. Sweat dripped from her face and she had her haired pulled back tight, which was something she didn't often do, due to her right ear. She had been exposed to radiation while still in her mother's womb. After several surgeries, when she had been a little girl growing up on the Moon Colony, all she had been left with was a misshapen ear that was red and shriveled; she couldn't hear out of it.

Devin approached to her right. His pants were wrinkled as if he had been sleeping in them, and his face sported several days' growth of brown beard. He had been traveling with her for a while now. At first she had tried to maintain her distance from him, but the loneliness of space travel had gotten the best of her. She didn't really know if she was in love with him or not. The last relationship she had been in almost cost her, her life.

"I brought you some drink," Devin said, holding out a cup of water toward her.

She pulled off one glove with her teeth and took the glass from him.

"I was hoping to talk to you about your friend."

"I told you before, Devin, I owe Colbosh my life and I'm going to help him, no matter what he asks me to do."

"What about me then, Michelle? I thought we had something going here. We had a steady job with the Zi-tec Colony, now we've dropped everything to help a fugitive!"

"He's not a fugitive!"

"He killed a whole bunch of people on Septis Four. He's a murderer, Michelle, he doesn't care about you! He's just using you for his own means! I won't stand by and let him destroy us!"

"You don't have to stand by!" she said, tossing the glass of water to the floor. "You can leave at any time. I'm sure some other woman will take you in. That's what you've wanted, isn't it? To find someone else?"

"Have you gone mad? What in the hell are you talking about? I'm trying to help keep you out of trouble, Michelle! This has nothing to do with me trying to find someone else!"

"Get off my ship!"

"I'm not leaving you! I just don't want you to ruin the rest of your life. Can't you see that I care about you?"

"If that's true, then you'll support me, regardless of my decisions."

"Michelle, please."

Couldn't Devin see that she was doing the right thing? Colbosh needed her help. If Devin wouldn't support her in this then he could walk; she would be sad that he was gone, but her debt to Colbosh was more important. Besides, Devin didn't seem like the type that would settle down with her; he was still too much of a free spirit. It was unlikely he would want to start a family with her.

"Are you trying to drive me away?" Devin said.

Was yes the answer to his question? Michelle thought. Was it what she wanted, though?

"Michelle?" Devin said.

Before anything else could be said, a chime echoed over the ship's speakers. Someone was hailing them. There hadn't been enough time for Colbosh to accomplish his mission, unless he had failed. The only other option was a security search.

"Attention crew of the *Elisses*, this is a random security search. Please lower your ramp and prepare to be boarded," said a male voice over the speakers.

Devin was standing next to her, but he was looking away and sweat was beaded on his forehead. Had it been there before? Was this a true random search or did the Earth security forces know that she had brought Colbosh here? They wouldn't have bothered with the random security search speech; they would have marched on board and taken them in custody.

The voice came back over the speaker again. "Lower your ramp now."

What was Devin nervous about? Michelle thought. Sweat started to run down his cheeks from his forehead and his eyes kept darting back and forth, like a caged animal trying to find a way out.

When Colbosh opened his eyes again he found himself looking out into another desert landscape. The twin suns were high up in the sky, but he could feel no heat, and smelled no smells. It was a virtual world. His droid hovered by his side, and when Colbosh turned around he could see the outline of small huts and sheds nearby. This was where the man they sought must be. For whatever reason this place existed in the mind of the person they sought; it had some connection to his own self-termination. Laws had been passed in many of the colonies including Earth to outlaw the death penalty. Now, the common practice was for the criminal to choose self-termination.

Humans had funny laws and even stranger ways of dealing with its criminals, Colbosh thought. His people would have sent the criminal out into the wilds without any supplies. If they survived more than a year, then they would be allowed back into the tribe. Humans preferred to lock their criminals up with other criminals and expect them to improve in behavior.

"I am receiving data streams from the programming, Owner. It appears that most of the inhabitants of the town ahead are centralized in a building, with the exception of one. There is a single data stream wandering out in the desert on the other side of town."

That had to be Reguilis, but why would he be away from the others? Colbosh wondered. What happened here?

"My database can find no reference of this place in the criminal's file. If we had some more facts about what planet this is and when these incidents occurred, I could find something from Earth's central database.

That is if this virtual representation is of an actual event or something once imagined in the prisoner's mind," Dim said in response to his thoughts.

Knowledge about what might happen here would've been nice, but this was just a simulated world; what harm could come to him here?

It was a short distance into the town. There were no streets, just alleyways between buildings, most of which had bullets holes in them and burn marks. In fact, several of the buildings they passed looked as if they had been burned out completely. Concrete barricades had been placed in several places between buildings. Most of the buildings they came across didn't appear to be inhabitable, not that they came across anyone.

On the other side of the town Colbosh could see a lone figure standing at the crest of a dune. This had to be the man they sought.

"Owner, I have been able to identify the man standing outside of the town. It is Reguilis."

At last he would have the answers to his questions. He would be one step closer to discovering who had hired Reguilis to destroy the atmosphere generator on his world. Then they, too, would meet his justice.

Reguilis wore a leather vest over a navy shirt and dark pants with a white stripe down the sides. He didn't notice their approach until they were right behind him. When he spun to see them, he fell to his knees with his mouth gaping open.

"Is it time, Demon?" Reguilis said.

Demon? Colbosh thought. What did the human mean?

"The definition of demon is often referred to as an evil spirit or deity," Dim told Colbosh.

"I tried to atone for my sins," Reguilis said. "Is there nothing I can do, Demon?" Tears were streaming from the man's eyes.

Colbosh growled at the man; if he had a weapon he would've placed it against the man's head.

"Please, give me another chance. I can save them this time, I swear I can."

What was the man babbling on about? Save who, and so what? The man would give him the answers to his questions or else".

"Owner, I have detected several new data streams entering into the programming. Their hostile level has not been determined."

One of the twin suns was setting off in the distance, and in front of Colbosh a cloud of dust billowed up into the red sky. Something was coming this way. Time was running short, and he needed answers now. He grabbed the man by his shirt and jerked him to his feet.

Tears poured freely from the man's closed eyes and his lips trembled when Colbosh growled in his face.

"My owner wishes to know who hired you to sabotage the atmospheric generator on Chevron Five," Dim said.

"I promise I can change things, just give me another chance. I don't want to go to hell!"

"If you do not tell my owner the answer to his questions," Dim said, "my owner will inflict pain on you! I do suggest you cooperate with us."

"Just another chance, I swear."

Colbosh slammed his elbow into the man's face and he went down on his back, gripping his nose with both hands; there was no blood, though.

The dust clouds off in the distance were growing in size; something was cresting a dune in the distance.

"Who hired you to sabotage the atmospheric generator on Chevron Five?" Dim said.

The man crawled up on his knees. "I can change, I can stop them!"

The dust clouds became shapes now. Several dune buggies were zooming toward them, humans piloting them. Reguilis stared back at the sound of the buggies.

"No, wait!" Reguilis said, leaping to his feet. He was waving his arms above his head when the first buggy passed within inches of him.

"Stop!" Reguilis said, running after the buggies.

Colbosh chased after the man all the way back into town. The buggies had been halted temporarily by the concrete barricades, but as he passed by one of them, several of the teenaged humans piloting the vehicle had climbed out to place hooks onto the barricade. Most of the humans had paint on their faces and they were screaming at the top of their lungs while pumping their AK-57s in the air.

"Owner," Dim said. "The data streams are changing. Someone is reprogramming the raiders to attack us!"

This was a virtual world; how could they harm him? Colbosh wondered.

Dim answered in response to his thoughts. "It appears they're sending a high voltage spike through the raiders' weapons. If one of them hits you, Owner, it could adversely affect your body."

"Alter the programming," Colbosh said in a series of growls. The raiders behind them were pulling the barricade away. There were now two other buggies behind the first.

"I am unable to comply, I do not have the ability to affect the programming here," Dim said.

One of the buggies loaded with teenagers passed through the now open barricade; they were speeding right toward him as one of the females heaved her AK-57 at him.

He rolled out of the way, and came back to his feet running. He was in the center of an alleyway between two of the burned-out buildings. It was a bad place to be as one of the buggies drove in behind him. He leapt into the window of one of the buildings and crashed through one of the crumbling walls to the back side of the building.

From there he was blocked by another buggy approaching him. There was another building on this side and he was stuck in another alleyway. The building directly in front of him appeared to be more intact than the one he had just left, and there was just enough of a lip on the side of the building that he was able to leap up and grab hold of it.

Gunfire leapt around him and he could see blue sparks impact harmlessly on the building around him. He forced his muscles to haul him over the edge of the roof. His droid was already there, ducked down low to the ceiling.

"The building Reguilis ran to is about twenty yards from here, Owner. It appears that not all of the raiders were sent to kill us. Some of them are attacking the building with all of the townspeople in it."

How can I get there?

"There are two more buildings directly ahead. You could leap from the rooftops, but then you would have about ten to fifteen yards of open space before you reached the building."

He had to try it. Lifting himself to his feet he took off at a dead run toward the edge of the roof and leaped to the other building across from him. There was more gunfire from below, but none of it came close. When he hit the roof of the other building, he continued his momentum. The roof of this building was cracked and slanted, but it was still strong enough to support his weight.

At the edge he leapt again, down toward the ground. There was a firefight going on between the raiders and the townspeople. The building was on fire and he could hear screaming as he hit the ground and rolled, right into one of the raiders. The momentum knocked the raider from his feet and helped bring Colbosh to a stop next to a buggy.

A raider with yellow and red paint on his face paid no attention to Colbosh as he snapped his neck. These were not the people that posed a threat to him, but that could change at any moment. He pushed past two more of the raiders and walked past the flames roaring in the doorway of the building.

"Reguilis is on the second floor, Owner."

The stairway was nearby and some of the raiders were in the building. Two of the raiders were in a room to the side of the stairway killing several men and women who had holed up in the room.

It was not important what happened here; the man he sought was obviously responsible somehow for what had happened to these people, and it was fitting that he would meet his fate here.

"Next room over," Dim said, floating past a dead raider and several men dressed in blue jumpsuits covered in blood.

When he found Reguilis, he was sitting in a room by a window with his knees tucked tight to his body. Sweat and blood poured from his forehead. His eyes were open wide, staring into the flames of the room—until he saw Colbosh enter the room.

"It's time, Demon!" Reguilis said. There was a pistol in his hand and he placed it at his temple.

The man couldn't sacrifice himself yet; Colbosh needed to know. He leapt toward the man, hoping to take the pistol from his hand.

"Owner, wait!" Dim said, but it was already too late; he was on top of Reguilis, and the man had taken the pistol from his temple and fired it point-blank into his chest. There was no pain, just a moment of shock, and then blackness.

Michelle lowered the ramp in the cargo bay. Three men dressed in chest armor and helmets marched aboard. One of the men had a scanner in his hand and was waving it about the place. Another trooper stood beside him, resting on the grip of his AR-517. The third man stopped in front of Michelle and Devin.

"I'm Lieutenant Gibson, Who is the registered owner of this ship?"

"That would be me," Michelle said throwing her gloves over to a corner.

"Your name, and do you have the registration for this craft? I'll also need to inspect your flight logs."

Routine inspections were never this thorough. Did they suspect her of something?

"My name is Andrea Michelle, and yes, I'm the owner of this vessel. For the rest of the stuff you'll have to follow me to the bridge."

Gibson looked back at the other two troopers. "Continue on with the scan," he said then looked back at her.

"Stay here, Devin," Michelle said. The sweat was dripping from his face now, as if he had been hitting the heavy bag instead of her. He hadn't even looked at her when she spoke to him.

"Devin?"

"I heard you!"

There was something wrong; was he going to betray her? What could she do about it, though? Gibson was following behind her as she walked down the narrow hallway toward the bridge at the end. If she turned and fought him, she might be able to take him out, but not before the other two troopers arrived. Like an idiot she had left her weapons in her quarters, which she would pass in a second.

She could dive in for them. That still wasn't a good option; there would be no way she could take out all three troopers before they alerted their command.

"Is something wrong?" Gibson said.

Damn, she had stopped at her bedroom door.

"No, just catching my breath." Gibson didn't even crack a smile.

Most of the lights on the bridge had been powered down to conserve on energy when she arrived with Gibson in tow. She took a seat at the main pilot console and brought the computers back online.

"I haven't seen a J-200 Series freighter since the war," Gibson said. "How have you managed to keep it flying?"

She ignored his question as she pulled up the registration file. "Here you go," she said.

Gibson stepped right up behind her seat and peered down over her shoulder. "Now I want to see your flight log, specifically the last couple of stops."

What was so important about her flight log? Gibson had to be looking for something specific, but what?

The computer was processing slowly and it took several minutes before the log pulled up on the screen.

"Sir," one of the troopers announced over Gibson's intercom. "We've found some illegal substances on board."

Gibson stepped back from her and raised his AR-517 toward her. "Stand up," he said. "Put your hands behind your back."

She did as he said, and when he cuffed her, he escorted her back down the hallway. One of the troopers was standing out in the hallway looking into the room. As they got closer she could see Devin down on his knees; tears were streaming from his eyes.

"Sir," the trooper next to the door said to Gibson. "The man in the room claims that a wanted fugitive by the name of Colbosh planted the drugs in the room, and he was holding them hostage until they arrived on Earth."

Devin, you son of a bitch! He had betrayed her and Colbosh to the C.E.F.!

"Does he know where the fugitive went?" Gibson said.

Colbosh found himself standing on solid earth. There was a light breeze blowing in the warm sunlight. There was trees growing in the distance to his left, and directly ahead was a village in a valley. He could see huts and buildings made from the local stones and trees; there were people of his own race walking about down below, but none of them looked his way. He was home, back on Chevron Five; his clan lived down in that valley and he wanted to be with them once again.

After taking one step, he stopped. Behind him was a distant thrumming sound. He didn't have to turn to know what it was, but he did anyway. Way off in the distance, next to a snow-covered mountain peak, stood the engine of his people's demise. It was a large funnel-like structure that stood miles high with billowing white smoke pouring from the top. The machine provided atmosphere for this planet; it was an experimental plant created by the humans.

Thunder roared in the valley, but it wasn't thunder. Fire erupted from the atmosphere processor. The large thick funnel disintegrated before Colbosh's eyes, engulfed in a massive wave of white smoke that grew and rolled like a gigantic wave in his direction. When it hit, it passed over him, but around him there was nothing left. Trees and grass-covered meadows were gone; only bare lifeless earth remained in place.

His village was no longer there; it was just empty rocks like everything else. He fell to his knees and began smashing his fists into the rocks until they bled black, and then he sat up and pounded his chest with a great wail. He was alone now.

Dim was next to the medical table, observing his owner's vitals. His owner was dying from the electrical backlash from the prison's virtual program. Joe was standing over by the boarded window closing the case that held the computer terminal he had been using.

"Joe, is there anything you can do to help my owner?"

"No! It's time for me to leave, droid."

"Please, you must help!"

Joe had the case in his hand. "Sorry, but the C.E.F has found us and there's no time!"

"Is there anything I could bargain with?" Dim said.

"No!" Joe said, stepping past the medical table and toward another door at the far side of the room.

Joe had left him no choices; Dim deployed a cannon barrel from beneath his armored shelling. The targeting system lined up on the man, and he fired a shot that grazed the man's arm. The case fell from Joe's hands and he turned back to stare at him.

"The bargaining stage is over!" Dim said. "You will help my owner, now!"

There was a brief blackness and Colbosh felt himself falling. That sensation ended when he found himself in front of the burning building in the prison system. Flames had consumed every inch of the building and there were dead bodies lying around on the ground.

A few feet away from him, kneeling on the ground, was Reguilis. His face was smeared with black soot and more tears were falling from his bloodshot eyes; when he saw Colbosh approaching, he let out a deep laugh. The pistol was still in his hands, but he didn't bother waving it in Colbosh's direction.

"I knew you would come back, Demon! I knew you would!" the man cackled.

Colbosh's droid appeared to the left of him as he came to a stop right next to Reguilis.

"Go ahead and take me! I don't want to live anymore!"

"Owner," Dim said in the back of his mind. "The C.E.F has been alerted to our presence! We must hurry!"

Colbosh grabbed the man by the collar and pulled him face-to-face with him as he let out a growl. Reguilis only laughed as he shook in his grip. The man's lips were trembling and tears dripped from his chin.

"I'm ready, Demon!"

"My owner wishes to know who hired you to kill his people on Chevron Five!"

"I was told they could wipe my mind, give me a new beginning!" Reguilis said.

"Who?" Dim said.

"My sins washed away by science."

"Tell us who offered to wipe your mind."

"I killed all of them, too, didn't I?" Reguilis said.

Colbosh growled again in his face; this time the man didn't laugh.

"You will tell us who?" Dim said.

"Frost, Admiral Frost."

Colbosh dropped the man to the ground. Frost had been a ship captain during the war. A highly decorated one at that, but what would've made him decide to kill off Colbosh's people? It made no sense considering that his race had helped the humans defeat the Artrans.

"My owner wishes to know if you're telling the truth," Dim said.

"Frost promised to wipe my mind, but when it didn't work, he sent me here. I killed all of them. I thought I was helping them, but I killed them all."

Colbosh didn't care to hear the man's confession; he had what he came for. In response to his thoughts, the scenery around him went black and then changed into the light over his head. He was back in the room in the Earth building, still lying on the medical bed.

Joe was closing up the case again and heading toward a back door. Colbosh sat up and pulled the wires from his body, including a needle that had been inserted into his skin; a tube ran from it into a bag next to him.

"Our business here is concluded," Joe said, pausing at the second door. He pulled out a small pouch like the one Colbosh had given him. He rolled several black marble shapes out on the floor and whispered something to them. They began to glow red as they took off at a fast roll. Some of them rolled into cracks in the wall while others shot out under the crack in the front door.

"Those should slow C.E.F down some," Joe said, standing up and picking up his briefcase.

Several explosions could be heard nearby, one of them just outside the front door, which sent it exploding into shards of splinters. Colbosh covered his face and felt some of the debris hit his arms. When the smoke cleared he could see a soldier in full armor laying dead inside of the doorway. Joe was already gone, through a doorway which led into another apartment. That was the way Colbosh left the building as more explosions ripped the place apart.

Outside of the building he took several alleyways for about a block or two, trying to get some distance from the burning building. In this part of town, there were a lot of humans huddled together near fires made from old canisters. Some had made furniture from crates and other junk. How humans could treat their own people this way was beyond his understanding.

Then again, when he was young and worked in the mines, there had been a lot of humans there, as well, humans who had committed crimes or were just down on their luck. Some had been decent, but most were violent and angry.

"Owner, I have sent a call for a cab a block up," his droid said.

Good, he thought. Soon he would be able to leave this place, but how was he going to be able to get close to this admiral? He would be well guarded.

At the end of an alleyway a yellow cab descended from the sky traffic above and came to a stop right in front of them. The back door popped open, along with a cloud of black smoke. It was citrus-smelling at first, but then it turned sour in Colbosh's nostrils. He had to cough at the smell of it.

"Where we going?" the white driver said with a cigar between his lips. It was night and he had dark shades on.

"The New York star port," Dim said.

The cabbie said nothing else; once he closed the door they were off, weaving through the sky lanes. Colbosh held onto the handles above his head and when they arrived at the star port thirty minutes later; he gave the cabbie his money and staggered out of the back. His lungs were burning and he felt like throwing up.

With her hands still restrained behind her back, Michelle knelt down beside Devin in her cargo bay. The ramp was still down and Lieutenant Gibson along with his two troopers stood around them. Gibson was talking to someone, but she could only hear what Gibson was saying.

"Yes sir, we'll hold tight here," Gibson said, then he pointed at Jackson beside Devin. "I want you to take a position out in the corridor. If you see anyone approaching, report it immediately!"

Jackson walked down the ramp and disappeared through the doorway that led out of the hanger where Michelle's ship was parked.

"What's going on?" said the other trooper, who was standing a foot or two to her side.

"I just want you to keep these two covered until more support comes," Gibson said.

Something wasn't right. If everything had been secured, they would've been escorted to a secure room somewhere in the facility, Michelle thought. It had to be Colbosh; he must have escaped. What if he was walking into a trap, though?

"Michelle?" Devin said in a hushed voice.

"Don't talk to me!"

"I'm sorry, I really am!"

"You betrayed me, and over what, some illegal drugs?"

"You two be quiet!" Gibson said.

There was no quieting the fury that raged within her at the moment. Devin's betrayal had been as great as Johnas's was. She had promised herself not to think of him ever again. Why did the men in her life have to betray her; even Colbosh was keeping secrets from her.

"Sir?" Gibson said.

Someone was talking to Gibson, but she couldn't hear what he was saying.

Gibson repeated out loud: "Suspect cornered, we'll hold for your arrival, understood."

Could they have cornered Colbosh? Michelle thought.

"Who's coming down the corridor, Jackson?" Gibson said over his mike.

Jackson peered back in at them from the bay door.

"Repeat, who's coming down the corridor?" Gibson said. Blood sprayed from the back of Jackson's throat as he collapsed to the ground.

"Jackson!" Gibson screamed, taking cover behind one of the metal crates in the cargo bay.

A figure dressed in a black trench coat walked into the cargo bay. The face was covered over by a black hat. It was Colbosh, but what the hell was he doing? she wondered.

"Take the suspect down," Gibson said, firing his weapon.

"No!" Michelle said, rising to her feet and slamming into Gibson. That didn't stop the other trooper from firing, though. Gibson pushed her to the side and she crashed to the floor watching the bullets tear into Colbosh, but the bullets weren't having any effect.

That's when the trooper that had been covering them went down. He no longer had a face; it was just a bloody mess as he fell beside her. Then Gibson went down behind her in the same way. Out in the bay she could see two trench-coated figures approaching the ramp. One had a weapon drawn with a scope and the other did not.

The one without a weapon dissolved into Dim, hovering in the air. "My owner wishes to know if you're okay?"

She nodded.

"Then my owner would like to know if you would get him out of here?"

"Just remove the cuffs first," she said.

CHAPTER FIVE

Admiral Frost received the summons to go to the bridge when the *Dauntless* came out of light speed. Just before walking out of his quarters, he took some more no-doze pills and washed them down with the remains of his coffee. The walk to the bridge was short, but he did have to pause in the narrow corridor to steady his vision. It would take several minutes for the pills to take effect, he had to remind himself, or at least that's how it had worked for the past couple of days.

"Admiral on the bridge," someone announced as he entered through the bridge door and began walking up the ramp.

Commander Julius was looking down over the railing at him. "What's our status, Commander?"

"There are still survivors aboard the *Georgia*. The *Yorktown* has already sent rescue crews to retrieve them."

Frost stepped up beside the Commander. To his left and toward the front of the ship, crewmen were at work at their stations, and through the parasteel window directly ahead he could see several of the fleet ships moving around them. Further off in the distance, he could make out a spec that had to be the *Georgia*.

"Any signs of our attacker?"

"No." Julius shook his head. "Our sensors are gathering data from the ship and the surroundings now, but so far nothing conclusive."

"What about our Allies? Have they arrived?"

"Yes sir, I've already been in contact with the Artran commander, Pon-ta."

"What did they come with?" Frost Said.

"Sir!" Ensign Gina said from a console nearby. "The sensor analysis of the *Georgia* is done."

He followed Julius over to Gina's side.

"The Artran sent two warships, three cruisers, and two eels, sir." Julius said.

"Our allies were feeling generous," he said.

There was a display just above Gina's head. A thermal image of the ship showed a lot of blue frozen spots, where the ship's interior had been exposed to space, but right in the center of the ship was an orange spot. There was another orange spot near the engine room.

"What kind of weapon could cause such massive damage to the hull?" Julius said.

"A powerful energy beam of some kind," Gina said.

"Were any electron particles left over?" Julius said.

Gina shook her head no.

"It has to be some kind of weapon we've never seen before," Julius said.

Where were the other ships that had accompanied the *Georgia*? He had sent ten ships to investigate.

"Any signs of the other ships I sent with her?" he said.

"None, sir," Gina said.

"Keep scanning the sector, Ensign," Julius said, touching Gina on the shoulder.

Frost started walking toward the back of the bridge where Ensign Rick and Ensign Rudy sat at their stations with several displays showing an internal view of the *Georgia*. Both ensigns wore headphones and neither of them looked at him as he came up behind them.

On one of the displays he could see a large gaping hole through the side of the *Georgia*'s hull. One of the rescue workers looked out at the stars beyond. He couldn't hear anything being said, but he turned his head to the other side. There was a gaping hole that zigzagged all the way across the interior of the ship.

Rudy was the first to notice Frost was there and he motioned for him to come closer. The commander was already at his side watching the displays, as well.

"Report?" Frost said, clasping his hands behind his back.

Rudy lifted one side of the headphones from his ear. "Lieutenant Harrison has reported contact with the survivors. Three men and a woman, sir."

"Are they in stable condition?" Julius said.

Frost eyes scanned over the displays. Several of the rescuers were setting up an evac chamber just outside of a doorway. This would allow them to go into the room and bring the survivors into a stable environment long enough for the rescuers to suit them up and get them to safety.

"Kevin reports that one of the survivors is in critical condition, but the others are fine." Rudy Said.

A tent-like structure ballooned up on the screen; when it filled completely, a light came on inside of the chamber. The display with Harrison's name printed on it, down below in the corner, was the first one through the tent. On another screen, Kevin looked back at the four other rescuers that had followed him into the tent; the last one through was zipping the tent closed.

Once that was done, Frost watched Kevin turn the handle on the door in front of him. The room beyond was lit by a small battery-powered lamp in the center of the room. All the survivors were huddled together in blankets. The injured one lay on the floor next to them with a bandaged wrapped around his head.

It was a miracle they had survived so long; it had taken the rescue team almost a week to reach them. Was it a coincidence, though they had survived? Frost thought.

He walked back over to Gina's station. The display of the thermal image of the *Georgia* was still up on a smaller monitor next to the larger one. Part of the engine room and this corridor had been untouched. From the images he had seen from the rescue workers, this made no sense.

"Admiral?" Julius said. He stood next to him and he squinted as he looked at the smaller display.

"Why, Commander?" Frost said.

"I don't understand, sir."

"Whatever attacked her left those people alive, Commander!"

"We don't know that for sure." Julius was now looking at him. His hands were resting on the back of Gina's seat.

"Think about it, Commander. You saw the amount of damage the attackers' weapons can cause. It's as we thought. The attacker has left the survivors behind to lure us here," Frost said.

"Then why haven't they attacked yet?"

"That's the part worrying me, Commander. Perhaps their sensors are greater than ours and they're just sitting outside of our range, waiting."

"I could send two of our light cruisers to do a quick jump," Julius said.

"Do it, Commander!"

Julius was already on the move, stomping toward the front part of the bridge issuing orders. Frost's wrist hurt from grinding around on it with his other hand. He hadn't even realized he had been doing it until he let go.

If he was right, then the attacker was waiting for them and they boasted of weapons far more powerful than he had ever seen before. But who where they and what did they want? Frost thought.

"Sir," Rudy said, looking over in his direction. "Lieutenant Harrison would like to have a word."

He found Harrison's display. The man was sitting in a seat in the back of a shuttle looking right across at one of the women survivors. The woman was thin and her body was hunched over in the seat. She had a full space suit on, covering her head and body.

"Put him on," Frost said.

"You're on, Admiral," Rudy said.

"Harrison, this is Admiral Frost!"

"Admiral, I would like to give you a report from our medical officer."

Julius arrived at Frost's right side, just behind Rudy.

"Go ahead, Harrison."

The woman straight across from Harrison started convulsing in her seat. Harrison was out of his seat along with two other rescuers. "Get her out of her suit! She's choking on her own vomit."

Frost watched as the other rescue workers pulled the woman's hood off and foamy white vomit spilled out from it. The workers wrestled the woman to the floor. Harrison stood up and backed away from the woman. The other two workers had taken control over the woman; one of them injected her with a syringe and the convulsions eased up.

"Harrison, what's your status?" Frost said.

"Sorry, Admiral. The medic is worried that the survivors have been exposed to some kind of radiation."

"Does he think it's lethal?"

"It's uncertain, Admiral," Harrison said.

Julius stepped away from him as a young African-American lieutenant talked to him.

"I'll have more medics at your disposal when you arrive at the *Yorktown*."

"Thank you, Admiral."

"Your team has done a good job, Harrison," Frost said.

Julius tapped him on the shoulder from behind. "Admiral, Commander Pon-ta of the Artran fleet reports that the eels are reacting to something unseen in space."

Was the attacker finally revealing itself? Frost thought. Did it possess some kind of cloaking technology that could deceive their sensors?

"Do the Artran know where this thing is?"

"Unknown, sir," Julius said.

"Commander, contact Pon-ta and see if you can—"

"Sir!" Rudy said. "Something's happening with the rescue team!"

Several of the displays now focused on the woman on the ground; her eyes were frozen open and one of the workers had his hood off and was pumping the woman's chest.

Had the radiation killed her? Frost wondered.

What happened next he couldn't tell; it was as if the woman vanished in a ball of glowing energy that replaced her. It was a large ball that seemed to take up several of the rescuers' screens. When it moved, it engulfed a person whole. The people aboard the shuttle were running away from the thing, but where could they go?

"Ship appearing in Sector Two Two One!" someone said from the front of the bridge.

When Frost looked out the parasteel window, there was a large ship of unknown design sitting out in space nearby. He couldn't make out a lot of details with the naked eye at this distance. The ship wasn't firing anything; instead, dozens of white orbs poured from the ship, heading toward Frost's fleet.

"Give me a status report, Commander!"

Julius was toward the front of the ship, hunched over a table display. Two other officers were standing on the opposite side of him.

"Our sensors are reporting nothing, sir. It's like that ship and those orbs are wraiths; they don't exist in our universe."

"All of them are dead," Rudy said from behind him. The screens were all static where the rescue workers had been with the survivors. "What happened?"

In the back of Frost's mind he already knew the answer, but it hadn't stopped him from asking it.

"They're dead!" Rudy said again; he kept glancing from screen to screen, the headphones off his ears.

"The *Yorktown*, sir!" Julius said. "Those orbs are ripping through her."

The helm maneuvered the *Dauntless* into a position to see the *Yorktown* through the parasteel window. The orbs from the enemy ship were joining in with the single orb that had emerged from the female survivor. That orb had burst out from the side of the *Yorktown*, and white vapor was jetting out from the exit point. When the other orbs joined in, they swarmed the *Yorktown* before penetrating the hull.

The orbs ripped into her as if the armor had been made from tin foil. What were they and where did they come from?

There was a bright flash from the parasteel window and the *Yorktown* was no longer there. Frost could hear murmurs around the bridge. The orbs were on the move again; instead of staying together they broke apart, tearing into his fleet. Julius was shouting orders from the display table when Frost stepped up beside him.

The table was displaying an overview representation of his fleet and the ships' positions. Julius ordered the

Africa, Alaska, and *Atlanta* to pull from the fleet and fully engage the enemy ship. The Artran fleet was already in action. The warships were moving in close to the enemy ship, along with the eels. On the display, the eels were just squiggle lines moving, but in reality they were living creatures that had been bred in space. The true origin of the creatures was unknown, but it was obvious they were once part of the ancient Artrans. Even the Artrans didn't know the eels' full origins, but the creatures obeyed them without fault.

"If we destroy the enemy ship," Julius said, never looking up from the display, "it may take the orbs away or at least cut their power."

"Are our point defense weapons having any effect on the orbs?"

"Unknown, sir," Julius said.

On the display the *Alabama* and the *Washington* were blinking red. The display didn't represent the orbs but the blinking meant they were taking damage. Through the window, the *Alabama* was to the left, just past the *Jackson*. The *Jackson* was firing at the orbs that passed over it, but it didn't seem to affect them. The *Alabama* was venting oxygen in several places.

The enemy ship on the display began blinking red as the C.E.F. ships and the Artran ships closed in and began firing. Then the Alabama disappeared from the screen. Two ships destroyed within a few minutes; they couldn't stand up to this for long, otherwise his entire fleet would be decimated.

"Damn!" Julius said. "Two more enemy ships have appeared."

On the display, both were approaching from behind, and although the display didn't show the orbs, they had to be coming. The fight was over.

"Commander, get my fleet out of here!" Frost said.

CHAPTER SIX

Colbosh lay back in the copilot chair on board Michelle's ship. A green fog surrounded the parasteel glass, but didn't move about the ship, since it hadn't moved in the last twenty-four hours. Colbosh was breathing heavy with his head rolled over to the side. A thin line of drool dripped from the corner of his snout. Dim, on the other hand, was floating by his side, not moving, until an encrypted message flashed on the display in the center of the bridge console.

It was the return message his owner had been looking for. It took Dim's database about a minute to decipher the message. According to it, his owner was to wait at a series of coordinates deep within the Golar Nebula. The Golar had never been fully explored; it was a vast nebula that messed with navigation systems and other electrical systems on board ships. It was aptly named after the first explorer that disappeared into it. Since then many ships had tried but had ended up disappearing and never heard from again.

His owner must be informed of the information. Through their link he sent a small jolt of electricity to his owner's body. It was not enough to harm him, but just enough to bring him out of his slumber.

Colbosh jerked his eyes open and looked about the bridge. He was alone except for his droid, who was floating beside him. There was a message on the display in front of his droid; this had to be the reason he had been woken.

"Owner, your message was received. Their return reply is for you to meet them at a specified set of coordinates deep within the Nebula. I strongly recommend against this action. The Nebula is far too dangerous."

His droid was right; the Nebula was a dangerous place, but in order to do what he must for his people, he would go without hesitation. Justice must be served.

With the sleeve of a jacket he had acquired from Devin's closet, he wiped the drool from the corner of his snout. It smelled of the human, as well as of Michelle. He hadn't liked the fact she had been mating with this man, but it wasn't his place to tell her how to live her life.

Besides, after Devin's betrayal back on Earth, Colbosh doubted that Devin would continue to be her mate. Colbosh would've killed him for her, but that wasn't what she wanted. Her plan had been to drop him off at the next colonized world they came to.

"Do I set the ship for the coordinates?" Dim said.

"No."

He couldn't risk involving Michelle anymore. He had already put her in enough trouble with the C.E.F. Michelle was smart and resourceful, though; on their flight from Earth she had used a secondary identity for her ship to bypass the cruisers floating by. She needed to be as far away from him as possible, especially since he was getting ready to meet the most wanted person in the galaxy. Not to mention that this person had an unsettled debt with him and Michelle.

It was better if he took an escape pod to the coordinates and wait from there. That way Michelle could get far away from him. He stood and approached the door when it slid open in front of him.

Standing in front of him with her arms folded across her chest was Michelle. The stench of alcohol emanated from her mouth and skin. Sweat was beaded on her face and her breath came in long gasps. Her hands were wrapped in black wraps.

"Are you going someplace?"

"My owner wishes to inform you that we are leaving your ship," Dim said.

"I'm not stupid. Dante is here!" Michelle said.

She was right, Dante was here, but only Colbosh was going to deal with him.

"We are going to take the life pod from the ship," Dim said. "My owner wishes for you to then fly as far away from this place as possible."

"He doesn't control me. I'll go where I want, when I want!"

"Dante is not the forgiving type," Dim said.

"You should've killed him before; he's not going to let you get close enough now. Besides, what makes you think he's going to help you?"

"Once Dante hears my owner's proposal, Dante will agree to help him," Dim said.

"Are you so sure? Dante can't be trusted; just look at what happened to his brother. I have every right to go with you. I, too, need justice served."

She did have a legitimate claim for justice, but it wasn't toward the right person. The death of Johnas, her lover at the time, was the result of several factors, one of which Colbosh hoped she never learned of.

"This is not the time. We must travel alone from here out!"

Colbosh took a couple of steps past her, but the argument wasn't over yet.

"I know about the tracker."

How had she found out? Colbosh thought. Not that he was to blame for it.

"That got your attention," Michelle said. "How long have you known about it?"

"My owner is not responsible for the device implanted in your body," Dim said.

She stepped up to Colbosh. "I've had time to think about it. Johnas wasn't a very trusting person. I'm guessing he had it put there so he could keep tabs on me. I'm guessing I'm not the only one of his party that got it, though."

He shook his head no.

"So he had Dante and some of the others implanted with one, too. That's how you knew where to find Dante, and that's also how you found me, when they were torturing Johnas!"

"Yes," Dim said.

A tear had welled up in the corner of her eye; the memory of her lost loved one must have been powerful.

"You know the hell Dante's men put me through. Why haven't you killed him for me, if you've known all this time?"

"Dante is very well protected. It would've taken more resources than my owner has at his disposal to rid the galaxy of the man."

"He took everything from me!"

Tears streamed from her eyes, and her head was turned from him, as if to hide the fact that she was crying. How could he get her not to come with him? She was a powder keg waiting to explode. She could wreck all of his plans with Dante, and he needed Dante to accomplish his next task.

"My owner promises that if you leave him as soon as he leaves the ship, if the opportunity rises he will swear on the lost souls of his clan to murder Dante. Would that be a fair deal?"

"No! I want to see him suffer, like his brother suffered and I suffered! I want to lock him up in a room, where he gets raped every night and where he hears a loved one suffering in the next room! A quick death is meaningless; he must be made to suffer!" Michelle said.

"I cannot promise you that kind of justice," Dim said.

Her face was red and puffy as more tears streamed down her cheeks and dripped off her chin. She looked him straight in the eyes. "Would you settle for any less, in your pursuit of justice?"

She had him there; he, too, wanted the responsible individuals to suffer a long time for what they had done to his people. If he could do it, he would make them suffer before he killed them. Michelle wasn't wrong in her wants, but all the blame wasn't on Dante. Justice had to be served to him, as well; he had killed Johnas before rescuing her from Dante's men. That was the secret he kept from her and the one he hoped she never learned.

"If you promise to do your best, then I'll let you go and I won't interfere. If you succeed, you must seek me out and tell me how you did it, but if you fail, I never wish to look upon your face again," Michelle said.

"Agreed," Dim said.

She nodded her head, then hugged him and walked past him into her quarters, closing the door. That was the last he saw of her as he navigated his way to the cargo bay. Devin was handcuffed to the wall; he was sitting on the floor next to a crate staring as Colbosh entered.

He growled at Devin as he passed by and the man tried to push himself into the box. It was obvious from the man's stench that he had been afraid that Colbosh would kill him for what he did back on Earth. If it hadn't have been for Michelle, he would've.

The life pod was on the far left wall. It had a small door that slid open and he had to crawl into it. His droid drifted in beside him and there was no more room; it was a tiny craft, designed for one person. There were several cans of food and other rations strapped into wire mesh on the wall. At the front of the pod, near the window, was a small set of controls. When the door closed behind him, Colbosh pressed the launch sequence and it lurched out into the Nebula.

From that point on, he let his droid do the navigating. He would miss Michelle, but it was for the best. There was little doubt that his quest would eventually lead to his death, and for reasons he couldn't explain, he didn't wish to see Michelle dead.

How long had it been since Colbosh had left the ship? Two, three hours at the most, Michelle thought, sitting in the pilot's chair of her ship. She was back in a pair of jeans and a blue tank top. Her arms hurt from her workout, but it felt good. She had promised him she would leave as soon as he left the ship. So why hadn't she yet?

Part of her wanted to set out and find Dante for herself, but then logic kicked in and she knew it would be a futile attempt. Navigating the Nebula was certain death. Somehow Dante had figured out how to do it, though. Dante was nothing better than a pirate, just like his brother Johnas had been. Johnas had a heart, though; Dante didn't.

She would give it another hour and then she would leave. Perhaps Colbosh would need her, but as far in as he had gone, he wouldn't be able to send a signal out to her. She could try and follow the ion trail the pod had left, but the Nebula would've dispersed it within a few hours. So she was stuck for now and didn't know what to do.

Just an hour, she thought again. Then she would leave for good and not look back. She got up from the chair and strode to the cargo bay, watching each foot fall along the way

Devin was looking up at her from where she had handcuffed him several days ago. A dark beard was growing on his face and he looked dirty, as well as smelled dirty. She hadn't allowed him to use the rest room, so he must have relieved himself in his clothing.

"Michelle, please!" Devin said. "I know I did you wrong, but this is inhumane!"

He had no idea what inhumane was.

"I promise if you let me go I'll stay out of your way, and when we land someplace I'll be gone as soon as the door opens!"

The strange thing was she didn't want him to leave. At this moment she felt the most alone she ever had in her life, even after the death of Johnas. She hated that feeling.

"I'm going to let you go. Go and get a shower and clean clothes, then meet me on the bridge."

"Thank you, Michelle, thank you! I promise I'll stay out of your way!"

He jogged away from her once she took the cuffs off, apologizing the whole way. Could she forgive him?

It had been several hours since Colbosh had left Michelle's ship. His muscles were already aching from the cramped space. How much longer would he have to wait here? Dim had informed him a while back that they had arrived at the specified coordinates, but was worried about the electrical storms nearby. They couldn't move from this spot, however. If they did so it might be impossible to relocate it.

The only way they had found it in the first place was the electronic buoy floating in the Nebula near them. It was letting off a signal strong enough for any ship close to it to use to navigate. Dante and his men must have put hundreds of these things in here. That's how they were able to navigate about the place. Others could try, but without knowing the position of the buoys any attempts would fail.

Dante was smart, but not as smart as his brother Johnas had been. During the war with the Artrans, Johnas had played a deadly game of successful hit and run, or so Colbosh had been told by some of his clan members that had served with him.

That was the past; he was here in the moment and he had to stay focused on the objective ahead.

"Owner," Dim said. "The electrical storms have shifted in our direction. Do I have your permission to move the craft?"

No, he thought. They couldn't move; hopefully the craft could withstand the storm.

It didn't take long before he found his answer. The storm hit the craft with a furry. Dim struggled to keep the craft right side up as he was tossed around inside it. Somehow they managed to maintain position with the buoy, at least until the electrical systems on board shut down from overload. Then the craft was swept away by unseen currents, with no life support functioning.

Soon his air would run out and he would freeze to death. Freezing would be the most likely death before he ran out of air. He slammed his fist into the metal of the craft as he struggled to maintain his balance. Perhaps he had made a mistake in coming here, but there had been no other option.

May the souls of his clan find him, he thought.

Michelle was seated in her pilot's chair when Devin came in behind her. He had on new clothes, he had shaved, and his hair was still wet.

"Reporting as ordered," Devin said.

"Please have a seat." He was attractive; even now she couldn't help but watch him walk toward her.

"Listen—" she had begun to say when the impact from something threw her to the floor on top of Devin.

"What hit us?" Devin said, helping her to her feet. Outside of the window she could make out a shadow of a ship with some kind of line streaming from it. She had waited too long here; someone was harpooning her ship.

"Buckle in," she said, throwing herself into the pilot's chair and slamming the thrusters on the control board.

There was a second ripping noise as another harpoon pierced into her ship. If she could get enough speed up, she could jerk herself free, or at least she hoped, anyway.

"The cargo bay is venting," Devin said.

She turned the thrusters to full and dove down and to the side, but the harpoons stayed in place. Turning the other way, she drove straight toward one of the ships that had her. It moved out of her way as her ship skidded off its side plating.

There was another ripping sound and a jerk as one of the harpoons broke free, but damage was already done to her ship.

"Fire in the engine compartment," Devin said, unbuckling from his seat.

All the thrust was gone; they were as good as dead in space. The only thing to do now was to prepare for boarders. When Devin left the bridge for the engine compartment, she went to her bedroom and pulled the shotgun from her closet. She wasn't giving up without a fight.

Colbosh didn't remember when he had lost consciousness. It had to have been just after his droid had told him his body was going into shock from the cold. There was no thought at that point that he would ever open his eyes again, except to look upon the faces of his dead clansmen. But instead he was looking up into the face of a bearded man with glasses on and foul breath.

"The Hunter lives!" the man said, stepping away from him. There was some clapping and cheering going on around him.

Where in the hell was he? Was this the place humans had often referred to as hell?

"Welcome, Hunter!" another voice said. It was a voice he knew, but it took his mind a few seconds to remember it was Dante's.

Dante was seated several feet away from him in a throne chair made of wood. People stood to the right and left of him. Tapestries and ornate rugs decorated the room, and instead of electric lighting, candles and torches were set about, lighting up the interior of the place. Dante himself was dressed in solid black with a thick wool shirt that looked and smelled as if it hadn't been cleaned in ages. Colbosh's droid was floating several feet away from him.

In the back of his mind Dim was rattling off possible escape routes and the layout of the ship. Normally, it would have been vital information, but he didn't intend to flee. He needed Dante's help to accomplish the next part of his mission and he was going to get it.

"I was afraid that you might not have survived, Hunter. Especially since we have some unresolved business," Dante said.

"There is no unfinished business between us," Dim said.

A familiar odor blew his way; it took his mind a second to realize the scent. Michelle was on the pirate ship with him. He took in a deep breath through his nose. Her mate was here, as well, but not in the same room. He followed Michelle's scent to the right-hand corner of the room. A large black man was standing behind her; there was dried blood on her forehead and her hands were restrained behind her back.

She wasn't looking his way; her gaze was fixed on Dante, with such hate that if she could have returned fire, she would have consumed the room whole.

"That is where you're mistaken, Hunter," Dante said, moving to the edge of his throne chair. "I seem to remember that you owe me for the premature death of my brother."

Michelle still had not looked his way. Would she ever trust him again if she learned the truth? Colbosh thought. It seemed inevitable at this point. Perhaps Dante didn't have all the facts.

"I did not kill your brother!" Dim said.

"Perhaps you were frozen for too long," Dante said. "It's somehow affected your memory. So I'm going to refresh you a bit. Some of my men had found my brother and his beautiful female companion." Dante's eyes drifted over to Michelle.

Michelle spat in his direction; it didn't hit him, she was too far away, but it did hit the side of a man's boots with long black hair pulled back in a ponytail. The man slapped her. She kicked her foot up at the man, but he sidestepped it and moved in closer with his fist balled up.

"Enough, Sandy," Dante said.

The man nodded his head and stepped away from Michelle. There was some laughter going around.

"You collected a bounty on my brother's head from the C.E.F. You ignored the bounty I had for him alive. Why was that, Hunter? Was it worth more than the C.E.F. paid you?"

Michelle's hate had shifted in Colbosh's direction as realization began to dawn within her. He had killed her lover instead of Dante's men, and he had collected the bounty on his head.

"I do not deal with pirates!" Dim said.

"But yet here you are, wanting my help for something. Tell me why I should help you?"

There was no more sympathetic look in Michelle's eyes; even her scent had turned acidic. She would no longer trust him. He felt a twisting in his stomach, like he might burst the remains of a long-ago meal out, but he ignored it like he ignored her stare. He had spared her life because he wouldn't collect the bounty on her head from Dante. Like his droid had stated for him, he didn't deal with pirates. It was that simple.

"My owner needs your help in killing your older brother," Dim said.

Any laughter or comments that had been floating around before were silenced now. Dante propelled himself to his feet and stomped toward him.

"You wish to kill my brother, the great Admiral Frost?" Dante said with a sneer.

"Yes."

Dante was a foot taller than Colbosh; he came to a stop right in front of him.

"For this purpose I will agree to help you just this once! After that if I ever see you again, I will have you killed!"

If Colbosh ever saw Dante again, it would be the last he ever saw.

CHAPTER SEVEN

Colbosh tried to extend his legs inside of the small box he had been placed in at the beginning of the trip. How long? He thought. Like clockwork, his droid, which was resting on his stomach, answered him through their mind link.

"Owner, it has been seventeen hours and thirteen minutes since we were placed inside the crate."

No wonder his bladder was aching; it had been seventeen hours since he had relieved himself. Both his legs were numb and it was hard to breath in such a confined space. The only light source was being provided by Dim. This was Dante's sick idea of getting some measure of revenge on him, keeping him cramped up in here for the entire voyage.

If Dante's plan worked, however, then Colbosh might be more merciful when he killed the man. Just a little, though; most of the ways Colbosh imagined killing him had been most cruel and slow. That was, of course, if he survived the current mission. Dante had decided to use Michelle's freighter to sneak into Frost's Star Base.

Once on board, the special crate they had placed him in would be delivered to Admiral Frost's ship, the *Dauntless*. According to Dante, it was well known that Frost never left that ship for long. His droid had laid out a plan of using the maintenance shafts to maneuver into position near Frost's quarters. From there, once the prey was known to be inside, Colbosh would strike.

The assassination would be quick. The real trick was how to get off the ship without being discovered or captured. Dante's part of the plan had been to infiltrate the security system of the Star Base and disable all the internal security systems. This would allow him to sneak back into the Star Base and escape, or so it was in theory, but as experience had taught him, nothing ever went as smoothly as planned.

"Owner, the ship has docked."

There had been a slight jar. He moved his legs and arms as much as he could, to try and restore circulation to them. His right arm kept brushing up against the AR-517 Dante had provided him with upon being locked into the crate. In his boredom he had checked over it several times; it was in good working condition and had a fully functional scope attached to it. He had also been provided with a pistol and several clips of ammunition for both weapons.

Of course, there was always the knife holster strapped around his leg. Many of his thoughts involved the knife when it came down to killing Frost. It was a much more delicate weapon with lots of potential to inflict pain before his prey finally expired. He doubted he would have time for that, though. If he was going to escape with his life he would have to act quickly and efficiently.

"I have accessed the Star Base internal database," Dim said. "I have not been able to access their security system. Internal sensors indicate that several armed C.E.F. soldiers are on board Michelle's ship."

Routine investigation, Colbosh thought. Dante wouldn't have risked coming here "unless" he knew for certain that they couldn't catch him. That was part of the arrogance of the man he could use against him.

"The soldiers are leaving the cargo bay. A team with a forklift has begun moving the freight out of the bay."

The crate jolted once or twice and he could feel it being moved. For several minutes they traveled, and at last it jolted some more as it was lowered. It didn't seem that it had been lowered all the way to the ground. Instead it felt like the crate had been stacked on top of something. Where was he now?

"Reacquiring location sensors," Dim said.

They had to have been moved off the Star Base for his droid to need to reacquire the network. That meant he was close to his prey; his heart sped up at the thought of the kill. Frost was the architect of what had happened to Colbosh's people. With his death, Colbosh's vengeance would be complete.

"We are on board the C.E.F. *Dauntless*. Sensors have not detected our target, but several humans are approaching the crate. We are currently several meters off the ground. A forklift is approaching behind the humans."

There was another jolt as the crate was lifted up and lowered. He could hear the noise of the machine outside. It made a roaring noise that deafened his ears. As it moved away, the sound of popping and cracking noises filled the crate.

"The humans are breaching the crate," Dim said.

This was an example of one of those things that hadn't gone according to plan. The AR-517 was gripped firmly in his hands; as soon as the lid came off, he would take out as many as he could. Perhaps one of them would have a maintenance ID on them.

Michelle tugged at the tight-fitting jumpsuit she had been made to wear. It had to have belonged to a male who was slightly shorter than her. The reason it had to be a male's was because of the stench and stains that remained on it, not to mention it itched like hell.

"Stop dragging your feet!" Dante said, twisting her arm a little tighter.

They were aboard the Star Base. Dante was leading two other men somewhere on the station, while a tall black man by the name of Karl was taking a larger group to another part of the station. She had no idea where she was or what was happening, but if she got the chance she was going to kill Dante.

Her hatred for him had not diminished any since the truth had been revealed about what had happened to Johnas. The look on Colbosh's face had confirmed to her that he had indeed been the one that had killed Johnas. She would never forgive him for that, especially by making her think he gave a damn for her.

"Shit! There's a guard!" Sandy said.

Sandy had long black hair pulled back in a ponytail. He had a gray cap on that covered most of his face.

"Price!" Dante said. "Engage the guard! Sandy, use your silencer!"

"Understood," Sandy said, reaching his right hand to the back of his jumpsuit. From the small zipper pocket there he pulled a pistol. With his other hand he brought a black tube from his pants pocket, and with both hands behind his back he began screwing one end into the barrel.

Price was talking to the guard and dropped his tool bag on his foot. When the guard looked down, trying to move out of the way, Sandy stepped up and placed the barrel to the man's side and pumped several shots into him. The guard collapsed to the floor.

"Bring him in," Dante said, pushing her on through the door. The room was small, but it housed several consoles that lit up the room with displays and lots of blinking lights.

Price had taken a seat at the console and began typing at the keyboard. Dante had forced her into a chair and now he had a pistol out, pointed in her direction. Sandy dropped the guard in the corner of the room and stood by the door.

"How long?" Dante said.

"These idiots haven't even changed some of the security codes since I left," Price said.

"I asked how long."

"Not long, my lord. I've already managed to bypass the station's internal security commands. They didn't find the back doors I had left."

"That's excellent news!"

Dante gave Michelle a grin, showing off his stained yellow teeth. If only she could take his gun from him, but what good would that do? The other two would be on her in no time and she would be dead.

The alarm system sounded in the room.

"Price!" Dante said.

"It's okay, my lord. I've taken out all their internal security systems. They'll be looking for us for a long time."

"What about the *Dawson*?"

The *Dawson*? Was that a ship? Michelle wondered.

"I'm having some trouble. Someone on board that ship has detected my intrusion."

"Is it going to be a problem?" Dante said.

"I don't think so, my lord—Wait! Shit, they're blocking my access!"

Dante motioned for Sandy to come closer. Then he leaned in and said something to him. It was very low, but what Michelle, did hear sounded like Dante had ordered Sandy to kill Price if he didn't achieve his goal.

Sandy took a couple of steps toward Price, who was struggling at the keypad. Sweat dripped off his nose. Sandy stood directly behind Price now and raised the weapon to the back of his head. Whether Price sensed it or not, he paused for a moment.

There was a clicking noise as Sandy flicked off the safety.

A violin played in the background, at first soft and slow melodies then increasing in tempo and speed. As Frost stood in front of his window onboard the *Dauntless,* his eyes were closed, but he could still see the images of those orbs—or the wraiths as some of his men were calling them—ripping into the hulls of his fleet.

What sort of weapon was it? Where had they come from and what did the enemy want?

The violin had increased in such tempo that his head nodded in concert, as if he had been a composer himself. Vivaldi was a master, he thought to himself as the tempo died down.

Before it could play out its track, there was a loud chime from the table in the center of his room. Someone was paging him.

Upon opening his eyes he could see the *Cairo* attached to the space station several yards away from him. There were several large gaping holes in the side of the ship. According to some of the reports Julius had given him, the *Cairo* had suffered massive internal damage, but the engines and life support had remained intact. Initial estimates of repair would be several weeks. It was the same for many of his ships.

The chime persisted. He turned and strode to the back of his couch.

"Open."

An image of Julius appeared before him. "Admiral."

"Go ahead, Commander."

"We may have a security breach. One of the techs in the lower levels thought he saw someone familiar," Julius said.

"Who?"

"The tech thought it was an engineer by the name of Price."

The name rang a bell; Frost had court-martialed an engineer named Price about a year ago for selling information to pirates. Price had been tried on board the space station and was sent back to Earth for his prison term, except the ship never made it there.

"How certain was the tech?" Frost said.

"Very certain."

If that man was aboard the station that could only mean some of his pirate friends were with him, as well. The real question was what did they want?

"I want that man found, Commander, and quickly!"

"Understood, Admiral." Julius had come to a salute, but before it ended the alarms in his quarters sounded and the red light built into the wall just above his door started to strobe red.

"What just happened, Commander?"

Julius had dropped his salute and was talking to someone. The projector didn't show Frost who, but it had to be an officer on the bridge of the Star Base.

"We've just lost all internal security control. Someone overrode the system, Admiral!" Julius said.

Without any internal security controls, anyone on board the station could move about at will, Frost thought.

"Find them, and get your internal security back online. I'll send you some of the technicians from the *Dauntless!*"

"Understood," Julius said, saluted, and vanished from the holo-table.

Frost took a step back from the couch with both hands clasped behind his back. What did his brother want? It had to be Dante who had planned this; only he would have the audacity to try something like this.

Colbosh could see the hand of the person who had begun tugging at one of the loose boards on the crate. Outside light was pouring in and it would be no time before he was discovered. If he could kill them all before they raised the alarm he might still have a chance at success. Taking a deep breath, he held his weapon ready to blast the first person to stick their face in.

That didn't happen, though; an alarm blared around him. At first he thought someone had discovered him and they were running away, but when his droid reported that they had moved away from the box and vacated the cargo bay, he lifted himself out of the crate.

This had to have been part of what Dante had planned for him, or perhaps the spirits of his dead clansmen were helping him to achieve his vengeance. Whatever the cause, maybe he had a chance now.

"Follow me, Owner," Dim said in the back of his mind.

His droid led him into a small hatch built into the side of the wall. There was a control panel next to it and all the keys were lit up in red.

"I have not been able to access the ship's internal security system. There's only a thirty percent chance I will be able to break their codes."

He had to find another way. He could use explosives in the door, but that would give away his hand. If only he could get to someone with enough clearance, he could use their code.

"I could overload a power conduit in the room, Owner. That would send some technicians here?"

"Do it!"

Dim floated up to the ceiling above, toward a blinking light. There was a bright spark and the bay went totally dark. The droid began feeding him digital images through their link as two technicians entered the bay with flashlights. He had hidden himself near the crate he had crawled out of and one of the men passed near him.

He grabbed the man, slammed his elbow into his face, and pulled him into the crate. The other man had been too busy talking and looking up into the ceiling to notice.

"Patrick!" the man said now, panning his light around.

Once the man had moved several feet to his left, Colbosh crawled back out of the crate and took the man from behind, placing the blade from his boot to the man's throat. Growling into the man's face, he could see the terror in his eyes. The man looked like he wanted to scream, but whenever he moved Colbosh dug the blade even deeper into his skin. A thin line of red blood was now dripping onto the floor.

"My owner wishes to know your code," Dim said, now floating in front of the man's face.

"Code?" The man said.

"Your access code for the maintenance shafts."

"Zero, zero, nine, nine, six, five."

"Thank you," Dim said as Colbosh struck the man in the back of the head with his knife; he placed the man in the crate with the other and went back to the shaft. His droid already had it open for him.

"The passage is clear, Owner."

He crawled into the shaft with the knowledge that soon his prey would be dead and vengeance would be satisfied. Nothing after that mattered.

Frost was still standing by his couch when another chime sounded from his holo-table. It hadn't been long enough for the crew to have found the intruders yet, or at least he thought so. Perhaps he was wrong.

"Open," he said.

Julius appeared before him again.

"Any progress, Commander?"

"Not yet, sir. I thought I would relay to you that Ambassador Lor'ta has sent you an emergent communication."

It had been a while since he had spoken with Lor'ta. What could the ambassador want? Maybe he had heard about what happened on Septis Four.

"Go ahead and patch it through, Commander."

The table went blank. The Artran didn't send messages by hologram; they preferred voice communication only.

"Lor'ta hears that our fleets suffered heavily."

"Some of our ships did take damage, but we still have a strong fleet, Ambassador."

"Lor'ta also hears rumors that a Nomad has survived the accident on Chevron Five."

"Those are just rumors, Ambassador."

"Perhaps. Lor'ta would be most displeased if the rumors turn out to be true. We thought you understood our agreement."

Why was Lor'ta so concerned about one Nomad? Frost thought. It made no sense; the Nomads possessed no real threat to them.

"I understood our agreement completely," Frost said. "If there is a survivor, and I doubt that, I will have him killed immediately."

"Lor'ta has no doubt about your word, Admiral, but Lor'ta feels that the time for his people and yours has come to an end."

"Ambassador!"

There was still only silence on the other end. "Ambassador!" The chime was going off on the table again. "Open," he said.

Once again there was no holo, but a female voice from his bridge answered. "Sir, a wraith ship has appeared just outside of our fleet perimeter!"

They were here; could his fleet withstand another battle with them? Frost thought.

"Admiral," Lor'ta said over the speakers again.

"Ambassador, we're under attack, can you send us some more ships?"

"Lor'ta has sent you more ships."

"Thank you, Ambassador. How soon will they be here?"

"They are already there, Admiral. Lor'ta regrets that our relationship has to end this way, but the galaxy will be better off without humans in it."

What had the ambassador said? Was he responsible somehow for the wraiths? His mind would have kept on reeling except he noticed the hellish shape of something standing in his doorway.

The red lights bathed the lizard-like alien in an evil glow, as if it had stepped straight out of the pit of hell. Drool was streaming from the corner of its snout. Razor-sharp teeth clapped at him as it growled. There was a shiny blade in its hands and it ran like a gust of air.

He had no time to scream.

Michelle watched as the man named Sandy held the gun inches from the back of the man at the console. Price was his name, or so she thought; he was working frantically at the keyboard. Whether he was aware of the man behind him or not, she didn't know. All she knew was that the man with the gun was looking back at Dante, as if he was getting permission to perform the deed.

It didn't matter to her if they killed him or not; what did matter was if she could use this diversion to escape. The door was several steps away; if she could push Dante down or strike him somehow, then she might have a chance.

Dante nodded his head toward Sandy. Sandy turned back to Price; for a moment there was a dead silence as if everything in the room had become still. She didn't want to watch the man being executed, so she focused on where she might strike Dante. She could kick straight to his balls, which should provide the results she needed, but the gunshot never came.

"I've done it!" Price said

"Do you have complete access?" Dante said.

"Yes, my lord. I'm flooding the *Dawson* with gas now!"

Sandy lowered the gun from Price's head and returned to the door. *Great*, Michelle thought. The opportunity was over.

Dante pulled a communication device from his pocket. "Karl," Dante said. "Operation is a go, repeat, operation is a go!"

"On our way, my lord," Karl said over the device.

"Come on," Dante said, wagging the gun at her. "It's time to go."

"Is this what it's all about? You came here to steal a ship!"

"Not just any ship," Dante said with a smile.

She couldn't help but stare at the yellow stains on his teeth.

"We're taking the newest and most powerful ship of the fleet. That'll put a black stain on my brother's career!"

"I thought you were going to help Colbosh kill him?"

"I've helped Colbosh as much as he deserves. The rest is up to him. Whether he kills Frost or not isn't important. I enjoy making him suffer; it's only fair for what he did to me and Johnas after the war. Frost is to blame for making me who I am."

"You were a bad seed from the beginning, and Johnas knew it!"

"Don't talk to me about my brother. I loved my brother, bitch! I just didn't like the way he ran things."

"My lord," Karl said over the device. It was the first time Dante had looked away from her since they had begun the conversation. She was glad of it; those green eyes of his reminded her too much of Johnas' when he was mad.

"What's your situation, Karl?"

"We've boarded the ship. So far no resistance, we took them by surprise. We're moving to the bridge now."

"We're on our way, keep me posted!"

Dante's green eyes locked with hers. "This time, no more talking. Now get up!"

Dante was the one who should have died, not Johnas. She would kill him; that she promised herself.

Colbosh kneeled at Frost's side, examining the wound he had delivered to the man's head. Blood spilled out, soaking into the white-carpeted floor. For days now his rage had been so focused on this moment, the moment he would kill the man responsible for the death of his people. But just as he had been ready to deliver the killing blow, there had been the communication between Frost and an Artran ambassador named Lor'ta.

Lor'ta had been partly responsible for what happened to his people. And Lor'ta was also responsible for the mysterious fleet that had been attacking the human colonies. None of it made any sense. His people had mostly fought with the humans during the war, but that was no reason for them to have been singled out.

What to do with Frost, though? If he killed him, he would have to go after Lor'ta, but Lor'ta was in control of something very powerful. If he kept Frost alive, perhaps he could use him somehow or gain some more information from him about Lor'ta. That was what he must do; he would keep the admiral alive long enough to learn more, then he would finish him.

"Owner, several troops are approaching the admiral's quarters," Dim said.

He couldn't take the admiral through the maintenance shafts. He would just have to carry him to a shuttle. That was the only way. Tossing Frost onto his shoulder, he held his AR-517 at the hip and marched toward the door, just as a human trooper stepped into the doorway.

"Admiral!" the man said before Colbosh shot him. The man standing beside him was so dazed; he didn't even have time to lift his weapon before Colbosh gunned him down.

Dim was displaying an interior map of this level of the ship; so far there were no other troops present. The elevators were just a few feet up. When he got in, he pressed the hanger button.

"I've tapped into the ship's communication grid, Owner."

He growled.

"The *Dauntless* has left dock with the station and is joining the perimeter fleet. More troops have been diverted to Frost's quarters. Our presence is still unknown, Owner."

The elevator came to a stop and the doors opened. He was ready; he smashed the butt of his rifle into the face of a young man that had been standing in the doorway. The man went down and the door closed again. He knew he should have shot him, but he might need the bullets. His presence would be known soon; hopefully by that time, he would be long gone.

The hanger bay was filled with technicians that ran away from him as soon as he started shooting. He killed maybe two or three before finding a shuttle. He strapped Frost into the copilot's chair then took his own.

"Troops have arrived," Dim said, floating behind him. "Five in number, and they're taking up positions near the elevator. I still have not been able to hack into their systems, Owner. I will not be able to open the hanger doors."

Display control room, he thought. The image of the hanger bay appeared before his eyes. He could see the troops spreading out and the control room several yards away.

"Lay down a suppressing fire here," he said, pointing at the troops near another shuttle.

"As you wish, Owner," Dim said as the cannon dropped from his underbelly. It spun into motion and the bullets began to fly, ripping into the other shuttle with lots of sparks.

Colbosh ran, keeping his head down low, and dove through the door of the control room. When he came back to his feet, a single tech was cowering behind the console. He grabbed him by the jumpsuit and pulled him to his face with a snarl.

The tech closed his eyes, whimpering, and sweat streaking from his forehead. It was at this moment Colbosh wished he could speak English.

"On my way, Owner," his Droid said in the back of his mind. He tossed the tech into the wall and the man curled up with his knees pulled to his chest, crying.

Why was it that some humans were so tough and others were weak? Was it a deficiency in their genes?

Dim floated into the entrance of the control room, a hail of fire pouring from its cannon. "I have only twenty percent capacity left, Owner."

Get the tech to open the doors, Colbosh thought, stepping up to the doorway. His droid was still feeding him the location of the troopers. Two were slipping around the shuttle; two remained by the elevator and one was coming at him from the far side of the bay.

When one of the troopers peered around the shuttle, Colbosh shot him in the leg. The trooper went down screaming. The other one fired a couple of shots in Colbosh's direction and began dragging his comrade away.

"Owner, the tech is too terrified! I cannot get him to respond!"

Try again, he thought. From the image he was seeing in front of him, several more red figures had appeared in the doorway of the elevator. Five more troopers were spreading out. The game was about over; he might be able to take out several of them, but not before they managed to take him down. If only his droid could get the doors open.

The image of the troops and the bay faded out; at first he thought Dim had gone offline, but then he saw something white and bright melt through the side of the cargo bay and shoot up through the other side.

He had to grab hold of the door frame as the bay began to depressurize. Things were flying all around, including his droid, which appeared to be having a hard time staying in place. The tech was holding onto the console, but his grip slipped and he went tumbling out of the room.

"Owner, I can get us to the shuttle, if you hold on," Dim said in the back of his mind.

The weapon was slung around his shoulder from the strap, and he let go with one hand to grab hold of his droid as it passed by. Then he let go with his other hand. At first there was a quick acceleration to the hole in the bay, but his droid managed to slow it a bit. Around him he saw several of the troopers being launched out of the hole, along with tools and equipment.

The hole was big enough to pilot the shuttle through, or at least he guessed it would be. Regardless, he had to try it. Dim crashed him into the ramp of the shuttle and after recovering he strapped himself into the pilot's chair.

The ship around him was beginning to tilt and larger objects like other shuttles were beginning to shift. One was sliding toward the hole as he maneuvered toward it. Hitting the thrusters, he felt the shuttle jerk and shudder as it scraped the hole the orb had made, but he made it out before the other shuttle blocked his exit.

Whatever those things were, they could wreck a fleet in no time. If Lor'ta was in control of those things, then no one in the galaxy was safe. But where had they come from? Colbosh thought. The Artrans had no weapons like that during the war. It was technology far too advanced.

"Owner, I have detected Michelle's signature in the ship leaving the system. Should I set a course to follow?"

Yes, he thought. He would follow Michelle for now. She didn't deserve to die at the hands of that monster Dante, no matter how she felt about him, now that she knew he was responsible for her lover's death. It was time to get answers. He hoped Frost would give them willingly because he didn't feel like cleaning up a mess afterwards. Pain could be such a useful tool.

He made sure all straps were securely in place on the admiral, and restrained his wrists to the arms of the chair before slapping the man twice across the face. The man stirred; when his blue eyes took Colbosh in, he tried to push himself out of the chair.

"Get away from me," Frost said. "Get away!"

His droid floated up in front of the admiral as he growled into the Admiral's face. The man recoiled as if he had been struck in the face.

"My owner wishes to know why you killed his people," Dim said

The admiral struggled at the restraints. "I didn't kill anyone! I order you to let me go!"

The arrogance of the man; did he really think he could order Colbosh around? He pulled the blade from his boot and brandished it before the man's face.

"I order you to release me, alien!"

"My owner, Colbosh, is no longer in the service of the human military. I suggest for your own well-being that you cooperate with him, admiral."

"I don't work with kidnappers, especially when my fleet is under attack! Now release me and take me back!"

"That is not possible, admiral, unless you answer my owner's questions."

"Do you know what you have done, Colbosh? I'm sure you do; I know all about your record. If you release me now, I might have the death sentence dropped. You'll do time—"

He dug the knife into the back of Frost's right hand and the admiral screamed out in pain and thrashed against the restraints once again. Once the screams began to die down, Colbosh pulled the blade free. Blood pooled out and began flooding over his hand and down onto the floor.

"Let's start again, Admiral," Dim said. "My owner wishes to know why you had his people killed."

The admiral's face was scrunched up in pain as he began to talk. His prey was not as strong-willed as Colbosh had thought. Soon he would have all his answers and then he would kill him. It was that simple.

CHAPTER EIGHT

Unknown world in wild space

Frost blinked twice before his surroundings came into focus. He was still alive, but why? The pain in his hand was still there, but there was now a bandage in its place. The only light coming in was from the shuttle's cockpit window. It was cracked, but hadn't busted out. Through the window he could see the bark of a tree pressed into the side of the shuttle.

What had happened? He tried to remember. The last thing he could recall was sitting in this exact same seat with the alien, Colbosh, demanding answers out of him. But now he was unshackled other than the restraint belt, and looking out into the scenery of a jungle before him.

Had the alien intended to take him here? Perhaps someone had intercepted the alien and they had crashed on an inhabited world. Whatever the case, he needed to get out of here before the alien returned.

His legs ached as he pushed up from the seat with his arms and forced himself to his feet. The shuttle's ramp was already down and he stumbled a bit as he walked out into the warm sun. So warm, in fact, a bead of sweat was already running down his cheek. Animal noises echoed around him, some familiar but not quite right.

It looked like any jungle one would find on Earth, but the noises were somewhat different, and when he looked up into the sky and saw three moons, he knew he wasn't on Earth.

A gunshot somewhere in the distance sent a flock of birds in a nearby tree flocking away, screeching. There were several more gunshots. It either had to be the alien or this was a human-colonized world. Given terrain like this, it had to be a human-colonized world.

He decided to walk in the direction of the shots; he had to find out if he was on a world with friend or foe. He hoped for friend, because he needed to return to his fleet as soon as possible.

It didn't take long for him to discover what he was up against. About fifty yards from the shuttle crash he discovered several men gunning down a young lieutenant in uniform. The badge on the lieutenant's sleeve looked like the circled symbol for the *Dawson*.

Frost kept his head tucked down behind a tree, near where the lieutenant had been shot. What was going on here? Was he on a pirate world?

Although the men who had shot the lieutenant were talking, he couldn't make out what they were saying. That was when he felt something near. Looking back he saw a long snake-like body with orange skin coiled up near his outstretched leg. It was hissing at him with its fanged mouth wide open.

He couldn't stop his scream as he rolled away from it, got to his feet, and ran. The adrenaline was pumping through his veins; he thought he had felt the snake strike out at him, but it hadn't pierced him. That was a good thing; the only problem was that the armed men that had gunned down the lieutenant were now chasing after him.

Michelle was seated at Dante's feet with her hands bound. She was still dressed in the same gray jumpsuit she had on during the heist, but the heist had been several days ago and she was more than ready to get out of it. The smell from the previous wearer was making her nauseous.

Several feet away from her she could hear people cheer as men from the *Dawson* were forced to fight each other in an arena. The particular fighting going on was between two young men. Both had a knife in their hands and both men were bleeding from several deep cuts. The taller of the men had been the previous victor.

"So what do you think of my little paradise?" Dante said, lowering his face toward hers.

"It would be much better without you."

"Is there really that much difference between me and him?"

His breath reeked of alcohol. "You mean your brother? Why can't you say his name anymore?"

Dante sat back in the wooden chair. "Johnas wanted to make amends with his older brother; Frost wouldn't have it. He always thought he was better than us."

"Was that any reason to kill him?"

"I didn't kill him, remember? Your friend did!"

She remembered well that Colbosh had acknowledged killing Johnas, but she realized, too, that if Dante would've had his way, Johnas would have died a lot less mercifully.

"At least Johnas had a heart!"

He smirked at her. "That's true. My brother did have more heart. That was his failing; it made him weak. I'm not!"

He was near her face again, breathing heavy on her neck. "So let's make a deal, shall we? How about you being my girl for a while, and I promise not to put your traveling partner in the fighting ring? I don't think he will fare too well, do you?"

What choice did she have? Some part of her still cared for Devin, despite what he had done to her on Earth. She realized now that he had only done it out of love for her.

"I'll take your silence as a yes." Dante sat back in his chair and clapped as the victor from the last round pounced on top of the other man and dug the blade deep into his chest.

She couldn't let Devin go through that, not for her.

A tall black man named Karl stooped over beside Dante's chair. Karl looked at her for a second, but then focused totally on Dante. She knew Karl; he had served with Johnas many years ago. In fact, he had been one of Johnas's most loyal men until Dante took over.

"What have you found out about our mystery guest, Karl?" Dante said.

"My lord, it was a long-range shuttle from the *Dauntless*. Somehow it followed us here."

"That's impossible!"

"It's not, my lord," Karl said, turning his head slightly so he was looking right at her.

"We scanned her," Dante said, rising from his chair.

"Price discovered an encrypted signal being transmitted from her body. Someone was activating a transmitter in her body this whole time," Karl said.

"It must be the Hunter. He's come for her!"

"We don't know, my lord. The one thing I do know is that Admiral Frost is now our prisoner. Some of our men captured him."

Dante clapped Karl on the shoulder. "Frost is here and alive?"

"Yes, my lord."

"That means the Hunter is with him; go with some more men and bring Frost back to me!"

Colbosh was alive and he was on the planet, Michelle thought. Had he come back for her? That made no sense; her life no longer had bearing on his quest to discover who killed his people. He had been certain that Frost was responsible, but it sounded like Frost was still alive.

"As my lord wishes, but what about the Hunter?"

"Don't worry about that, Karl. I have something planned for him. Just get Frost back to me!"

Karl bowed once and took off at a run.

Dante squatted down next to her. His nose was almost touching hers as he spoke. "How sweet. Your alien lover has come to save you."

"He's not here for me!"

Dante rubbed his nose against hers. At first she recoiled from him, but he grabbed her and pulled her back close. His grip was hard on her arm and it hurt.

"You're right, I don't think he's here for you. I think he's here for me, but what he doesn't realize is that I have something special for him!"

He brushed his lips against hers and it took all the will power she could muster not to back away from him.

"Come with me," Dante said, standing up.

He helped her to her feet and led her toward the back of the old structure and down a flight of stairs made of stone. The lower level of the place was lit only by torches. Dante came to a stop next to a barred door.

Inside the room she could just make out an outline of two beings. There were growls and clicking noises coming from the darkness, similar to the sounds Colbosh made.

Were there Nomad survivors in there? She wondered.

"What is it this time, Dante?" A human voice said from inside.

"I've come to make a deal, Suntol."

Which one was Suntol? Was he human or a Nomad?

One of the outlines stepped closer to the bars; a green-skinned lizard like Colbosh smashed up against the bars with a snarl. Dante had to drag her back away as the Nomad clawed at them.

"We don't like your deals!" Suntol said, still in darkness.

"I think you might like this one," Dante said. "What if I told you that a Nomad from the Alar Clan is here on the planet."

The Nomad at the bars kept clawing at them.

"Alar is our sworn enemy," Suntol said.   "The ancient hates should be swept away. I will have no part in this."

"What about your clansman here, Suntol? I think he would be willing to do it for me if he was promised a shuttle off this world."

"I won't help you!"

"Have it your way." Dante stepped away and pushed her along with him.

"Wait," Suntol said. For the first time Michelle could see him. He was a Nomad, as well, but his skin had turned brown with large black spots on the skin. There were scars around his throat, but he walked as tall and as straight as the other Nomad.

"I will tell my clansman your offer, but I will not go!"

Dante nodded his head in approval. Suntol's voice changed to a series of growls, grunts, and a few clicks of his tongue. It was hard to believe that this Nomad could speak English. Perhaps those scars around its neck were from surgeries.

It hadn't been uncommon during the war for Nomads to have undergone experimentation, she thought. Colbosh was living proof of that.

"My clansman agrees to help you find and kill the other."

"Excellent, Suntol. I'll send someone down in a minute to release him."

Dante grabbed Michelle by her restraints and pulled her along with him back up the stairs. "Come along, my love, I have one more surprise for your friend. Something that was left here thousands of years ago. I'm sure you'll find it quite amusing."

Deep down in her heart she hoped that the only reason Colbosh had come here was to kill Dante.

Colbosh sat high up in the treetops looking down at the pirates who had captured Frost. There were three all together, with a mixture of weaponry, some with rifles and others with pistols. Dim had reported to him that their alcohol levels were high. That was a bonus in his favor. The only problem was his droid had reported that more pirates were en route.

Dim had given him a pretty good layout of the place. There was a valley about a mile to the east. To the north there was a structure of some kind. His droid had reported that the structure was the main pirate base. He would be able to sneak past the pirates out in the woods, but once in the base he would be more exposed. His droid reported at least two to three hundred individuals in the structure. That had to be a combination of Dante's pirates and perhaps the surviving crew of the *Dawson*.

"Owner, four more pirates are nearing the admiral."

The life of the admiral wasn't important to Colbosh. The only reason he had spared his life in the shuttle was because he needed the admiral to help him find the Artran ambassador. The admiral had access to things he never would be able to get to; it was his only chance.

Through the scope of his AR-517 he had acquired on board the admiral's ship, he could see a tall black man with three other well-armed men approach the other pirates holding the admiral hostage.

He needed some kind of diversion. His droid could use the holo projector again while Colbosh picked them off from the treetop. Which to kill first? The tall black man was definitely in charge; the other men were doing what he ordered them to do. If Colbosh picked him off first it would definitely throw them into chaos, but that might lead them to grab up the admiral in defense, or even kill him. If he didn't kill the black man first then he might keep the men organized enough for a counterattack.

He lined up the crosshairs square on the black man's head. His droid was already moving toward the pirates. One of the pirates next to the black man noticed Dim. They began taking cover and firing. He pulled the trigger and the black man's skull burst open like a melon.

As he had predicted, the men were in such disarray that some took off running into the woods while one of the more leveled-headed ones took cover behind the admiral. That was the one Colbosh took out next. The admiral collapsed to the ground, covered in blood.

"Owner, I have detected the presence of another Nomad approaching."

Colbosh missed what his droid said as he dropped another one of the pirates. Three remained and they were now firing up into the treetops as well as at his droid. Colbosh kept ducked in tight to the tree as the bullets whizzed around him.

"I am taking damage," Dim began to say before the droid's presence emptied from his mind with a buzz of static and then silence. Colbosh peered around through the scope and found his droid collapsed to the ground with smoke billowing from it. Near it, peering up into the trees was another one of his race. Taller and leaner than Colbosh, the wind was blowing in the wrong direction for him to get a scent of him, but scarring on the Nomad's arm told him that he wasn't of the same clan as Colbosh.

The pirates were continuing to fire at him in the tree; he now had no choice but to get down. Leaping from the branch, he landed on his feet and rolled away. When he came back up to his feet, he dashed behind another large tree and peered around the side. If his droid had still been active, he would've known where to fire without even looking, but that was no longer an option. It was the old-fashioned way now.

The pirates were still firing in a disorganized state, some still at the treetops. The other two were firing at the other Nomad who had entered the firefight. Lining up the crosshairs, Colbosh killed another pirate. The other Nomad also claimed one with a good shot through the man's chest. The lone remaining pirate rushed off into the jungle. Frost still had his head buried on the ground.

It was now Colbosh and the other Nomad. The wind was still blowing against him, so he still couldn't get a scent; but he heard some branches break nearby. He threw himself from behind his tree and rolled near another tree as bullets ripped out behind him.

When he got to his feet, he caught a glimpse of the other Nomad taking cover behind a tree several yards away. He flipped the switch on the rifle from single-shot to multi-fire. Now it was a matter of waiting the other out, but the longer he waited the more pirates would arrive. He had to finish this now.

The other Nomad peered around the tree and Colbosh fired several rounds as he rushed from his cover. The other nomad had anticipated his movement and was firing around the other side of the tree. One of its bullets hit him in the leg and he went down. He was close enough to a tree to crawl behind it. His leg hurt badly but when he looked at it, all he saw was blue goo oozing from his armor. It had protected him, but the impact still hurt.

The wind had changed; he could now smell the other nomad and it was closing in fast. He fired a couple of blind shots from beside the tree; he couldn't tell if he had hit anything or not but he needed time to switch out weapons. His AR-517 was running low. When the gun clicked he dropped it to the ground and pulled the pistol from the side holster built into his armor.

The other Nomad was screaming out his clan name to Colbosh in his native language. It was Orbo, a clan that his had been feuding with for generations. Where had this Nomad come from? Was it working with the pirates?

He looked around the side of the tree; he needed to move but his leg was stiffening up on him. His eyes caught movement of something to his left, and it took his senses a second to realize that the other Nomad had flanked him. A bullet hit him in the side and he collapsed to the ground.

Within seconds the other Nomad was on top of him. It no longer had a gun in its hand; it had pulled a blade from its belt and was leaping down toward him.

It took all of Colbosh's strength to keep the blade away from his throat. The other Nomad was growling into his face as the blade inched closer and closer. He tried to twist the enemy off him, but the pain in his side zapped his strength.

The tip of the other's blade pierced his neck. He was losing; all his strength was gone. His quest was at an end.

A gunshot rang out and it startled him. At first he closed his eyes in anticipation of the killing blow. When he opened them again he saw the black eyes of the other Nomad glaring down into his. Blood drooled from the corner of its snout as it continued to growl at him before it collapsed on top of him, dead.

The smell of the admiral was nearby; when Frost came into view he was standing above Colbosh with a rifle in hand.

"Why, alien? Why did you spare my life?" Frost said.

The admiral's face was smudged with black dirt and his arms shook as he held the rifle level with Colbosh's head. Without his droid there was nothing he could say to the man, not that it really mattered. Frost would figure it out in time. There was a strange smell of smoke in the air; he hadn't noticed it until now.

Frost looked off into the forest as several four-legged animals rushed past them. He could've used the distraction to shoot the admiral, but the fight with the other Nomad had robbed him of his weapon.

"I forgot you couldn't talk without your droid. I should kill you."

Colbosh growled at the man. If Frost was going to kill him, then he should do it now and be done with it. The smoke was growing stronger. More animals rushed past them as the admiral's attention was drawn toward the smoke.

"I know you can understand me. Get up," Frost said, motioning with the end of the rifle.

Their roles had been reversed. Why was the admiral sparing him?

"I don't know your reasoning for sparing my life, alien, but I need your help to escape from this place."

He pushed the fallen Nomad from his body and got to his feet. He could've rushed the admiral, but the admiral needed his help. Colbosh would make the admiral think he was going to help him, but in the end he would still use the admiral to reach the Artran ambassador. That was the only thing that mattered.

"Do you agree to help me?" Frost said. "Shake your head yes or no."

He nodded yes.

"Do you know how to get us away from this forest fire?"

He nodded again. From off in the distance he could hear the flames cracking some of the trees, but there was another noise, too, a faint mechanical sound that rumbled the ground beneath him.

"Pick up your weapons, but stay ahead of me," Frost said.

He did as he was told. He found his pistol nearby and he placed it in the holster on his armored jumpsuit. The smoke was all around them now and the only route away from it was toward the cliffs. The fire was spreading quickly, though, and it might consume them before they reached there. If Colbosh's droid had been active, he would know precisely how big the fire was and in what direction it was going. That wasn't an option available to him any longer.

He grunted at the admiral and set off at a steady pace into the jungle.

Dim's eyes blinked back on and he slowly rose off the jungle floor. Bugs and dirt covered him, but with a few twirls upside down, they came off. His systems had rerouted themselves around the damage but some of his operations, such as the link he shared with his owner, were not functioning.

His visual sensors could not detect his owner. They did, however, pick up the dead remains of the other alien of his owner's species. He found his owner's gel blood all over the corpse. He would have tried following the blood trail, but his threat sensors alerted him to a new and extremely large hostile presence. Floating behind some brush, his visual sensors made out a large spider-like machine smashing through the forest. The tracking device his owner had installed in the human female, Andrea Michelle, was registering from it.

The full capabilities of his sensors were not yet operational, and in their limited state he could not pick up his owner's location.

The tactical database gave several possibilities from the evidence at hand. First, his owner was probably already dead somewhere in the jungle. Second, his owner was a captive on board the alien machine. Third, he was running from the attackers. The possibilities rolled on. In a final analysis of his choices, the database determined that Dim was to locate Michelle. Since she was within reach, his owner would find him through her.

Dim waited for the thing to get closer, and without any kind of threat, he flew up from his hiding spot and entered into a small, round access port of some sort in the spider-like thing's belly. His sensors determined that it led to the interior.

Several kilometers into the shaft, he came to a barred grate blocking access into a room. His sensors also detected a human male presence. His visual sensors caught a glimpse of the man's head as he walked past. For a brief second the man glanced in, but he kept on walking.

The tactical database warned that Dim should find an alternate route into the interior. He was complying with the command when the shaft behind him closed. His visual sensors detected the man again. He was peering into the shaft.

Michelle found herself restrained in a form-fitting seat that pressed against her body. She was on board a war machine of some kind, but nothing like she had ever seen before. It had to have been a relic left behind by the Ancients. In fact she just now had begun to realize that the entire base Dante was using had to have been constructed by the Ancients. The large stone blocks they used in their construction hadn't registered in her mind until now, not that she had ever seen one of their structures up close and personal until now. Most of her knowledge about them had come from documentaries she had watched as a youngster.

"Test fire of the incinerator was successful, my lord," Price said.

"How do you like my toy?" Dante said, sitting in a chair raised up a foot behind her.

The man named Price was seated in a control chair next to her and he kept glancing over at her with a stupid smirk on his face. The man couldn't have been more than twenty years old.

"I asked you a question." Dante's eyes narrowed at her as he spoke.

"It's wonderful," she said, hoping that it sounded convincing enough to keep him from trying to talk to her more. The very sound of the man's voice made her tighten up as if someone had run a nail across a chalkboard.

"I'm glad you approve of it, because in another year or two we'll be able to manufacture it. Can you imagine it? A relic like this left behind by the Ancients with all of its knowledge and secrets still intact. I could take a dozen worlds with just a handful of these things."

"You're so delusional. Johnas never would've used this against innocent civilians. Johnas just—"

Dante pressed the release of his harness with a quickness she had never seen before, spun her seat around, and slapped her hard across the cheek. It stung badly and it made tears well in her eyes.

"Enough about my brother. How many times have I told you that? He's insignificant to what I'm going to accomplish. I will one day rule the entire Colonial colonies."

Hate kept her eyes focused on Dante's. She looked forward to the day that someone plunged a dagger deep into the man's chest and she prayed that person would be her.

"My lord, we're closing in on the last signal we received," Price said.

Dante had reseated himself and didn't bother to reattach his harness. He slouched down in the chair with a smile on his face. "I must thank you."

"For what?" she said.

He clapped his hands together in front of his face and held them there with his fingertips pressed firmly together. "For providing me a way to find the Hunter. I wasn't convinced that my men would be able to stop him, or the other alien, but with the firepower of this thing in my control, I can level the entire forest to reach him."

The transmitter in her body—they must have found a way to trace it back to the source, Michelle thought.

"My lord," Price said. "The other alien's body, along with some of our men, are here, but no sign of the Hunter."

"What about the signal?"

"It just went blank several minutes ago. Perhaps the hunter realized we were using it against him," Price said.

"That's unlikely. Spread the fire in a further arch. I want to keep him pinned in."

Price's lip trembled as he glanced at her and then back at Dante. "My lord, we might not be able to control the fire if we spread it further. What about our base?"

Dante slapped his palms down on the arms of the chair and sat at the edge. "Do it, Price. Now."

Price turned back to the control board with his upper teeth digging into his lower lip. Dante was insane; he would risk killing his own people just to kill Colbosh. What kind of monster had Dante become? She thought.

The smoke made Colbosh cough and bend over at the waist, struggling to take in a clean breath. Smoke was all around him and the admiral. The human had kept up with him, but he, too, had succumbed to the smoke now. Visibility had grown to almost zero, but the closer they came to the cliffs the more the smoke abated.

"We must go down," Frost said, slinging the rifle over his shoulder and lowering his right foot down to a small outcropping of rocks in the cliff.

The rumbling beneath Colbosh's feet was growing stronger and trees could be heard cracking and popping, not from the fire but from something massive that was tearing them from the very ground. He couldn't see it through the haze, but he could sense that it was closing in on them. He had hoped not to have to take the cliffs, but there was no other option now.

"Come on," Frost called up at him.

The human was making good progress. The upper part of the cliff provided enough handholds and supports to progress down without much effort, but halfway down toward the river below was another thing.

He had caught up with Frost, who was sweating profusely and was panting for breath, looking down like a desperate man. "I don't think I can go any further," Frost told him.

Colbosh fingers were beginning to ach from the strain and further down didn't look to be any good footholds. The cliff started curving inwards.

"Go ahead. I'll see what I can do," Frost said.

A deep burning sensation was spreading in his arms as he dangled down and he still had several more kilometers to go before reaching the bottom. Up above, the human was still moving along well, but he could tell that the man's strength was zapped. He was taking in long rasping gasps for air and his arms were trembling.

In his mind it was likely that the human would fall to his death, a fair and natural judgment of nature. Justice would be served and he would find another means of reaching the Artran ambassador. By the same token, however, he could feel his own arms failing. Nature might claim his own life, as well.

That couldn't be his fate; justice for his people had to be served. The souls of all those avenged would give him the strength he needed to succeeded, he was sure of it.

From up above pebbles and rocks began to break loose from the top of the cliff. Some of the pebbles pelted him on the shoulders and back. Due to the natural arch of the cliff, most of the larger stuff flew on past, plummeting into the river below.

"What the—?" Frost said as more rocks tumbled down.

From the edge of the cliff above Colbosh could see a pair of long mechanical legs appear from over the edge of the cliff. They dug down hard into the side, penetrating so deep into the surface that the rocks around him shook.

It took all of his strength to keep his hands firm on the holds he had. The body of the thing soon appeared over the side, as well; it was semicircular with a large orange canopy that peered down at them. A barrel at the lower base of the body began to glow white.

It was too far to jump to the river below; even if he did, he would probably break several bones in the swells and drown. Nature wasn't going to be his death. It was this abomination lurking above him.

The smell of smoke had entered the cockpit of the machine Michelle found herself captive in. Beyond the orange canopy she could see fire licking all around, engulfing trees and fauna. It was likely that in Dante's quest to kill Colbosh he would kill himself and her in the process.

"I found them, my lord," Price said. "There, climbing down the cliff."

"Excellent."

Michelle watched as two of the machine's feet disappeared over the edge of the cliff facing. A minute later the body followed and she was now looking down toward the river and two figures way down on the side of the cliff. It was too far to make out any features, but the one closer to the bottom looked like Colbosh.

"Kill them, Price, kill them now," Dante said, slapping his palms on the armrests again.

What could she do?

"As you wish, my lord." Price began pressing buttons on the control board.

Michelle wanted to yell out, jump, but no one would hear her.

Fire began to spray out from the nozzle of the spider's body. It was too late, she thought, but just as it had begun, it stopped. Price pounded his fist on the console in frustration, only for it to explode in an arc of electrical discharge that surged through his body.

When it ended, Price still sat with his head slumped over, smoke plummeting from his body and a steady stream of blood drooling from the side of his open mouth.

From behind her she heard Dante scream out something, but by the time she turned to see what had happened, Dim floated to her side with a mechanical arm outstretched from its armored body. There was several surgical instrument attached to the arm, but the one in use was a long syringe. It receded into some kind of sheath in the arm and disappeared into its armored shell.

"My owner will find me through you," Dim said. There was a bullet hole in its armor.

"Are you okay?" She said not certain if she should even ask.

"My owner will find me through you."

What could she say to a machine? "Your owner is down there, and if you release me, maybe I can help you."

"Owner," Dim said, floating away from her as the canopy hissed and cracked open partially around her. How had the droid gained such complete control over this machine in such a short time? The important problem at the moment was how could she free herself from the restraints and help Colbosh get up here.

The canopy continued to rise around her with a thrumming noise. Dim had taken a position next to Price's lifeless head, and she thought about asking the droid to let her go again when the machine began to move. The seat gripped into her body as the legs dug into the cliff and began descending.

At any moment she half expected the thing to topple over and go plummeting into the river below. About halfway down the droid lowered the body of the machine as close to the surface of the cliff as possible. Frost was above Colbosh. The admiral's face was stained in dirt and grime, mixed in with sweat. He was breathing hard as he found handholds to help him climb into the cockpit of the machine.

The admiral looked nothing like his brothers. Both Dante and Johnas had short and curly hair. Frost had straight dark hair, and wasn't as broad in the shoulders.

"Could you untie me?" she said as Frost looked up at her from the floor of the canopy.

"Is he dead?" Frost asked, looking past her at Dante.

She shook her head at first. "No, I think Dim injected him with something. The man beside you is dead, though."

The admiral took a second to glance at the body before crawling closer to her. "One less traitor in the galaxy," he said.

"Is that what you thought of Johnas?" She didn't know why she said it

He stopped pulling at the restraints and looked at her. "What I think about Johnas is up to me." Then he went back to the restraints, and one of them broke free. She was moving her arms as Colbosh climbed over the side of the canopy. His body, too, was covered in grime, along with long streaks of the gel-like substance in his armor. She could see several places where he had been hit. It didn't look like he was bleeding anywhere, but the impact from the bullets had to have taken something out of him.

"Owner," Dim said. "What are your orders?"

Colbosh wouldn't look at her; he had turned his body so he wasn't even looking in her direction. She was glad to see him alive, but she wasn't happy that he was near her. He had murdered Johnas, and the man releasing her from her restraints had placed the bounty on his head that Colbosh collected. Everyone she should hate was within striking distance of her.

Dim said, "Owner, the nearest shuttles are about twenty kilometers to the west. There is a large contingent of armed men there. I do not have a full tactical listing for you."

"It must be Dante's base," Frost said. "Some of the crew from the *Dawson* must be there. If we could free those men, they could help us."

The conversation brought her out of her thoughts temporarily. In order to survive this she was going to have to work with them, no matter her feelings. It wasn't an easy thing to ignore her hatred, but she had done it before in the past, especially when it had been focused on Dante. Now she knew the truth.

"Dante has the crew members locked up in the prison block in the lower levels of the base. He's been using them for his amusement," she said.

"Is it all of the crew?" Frost said.

"I don't think so. There were only two other cells beyond the one I was taken to and they weren't too big."

"So he must have only brought down some of them. That means he probably left the rest on board the ship in space. That could work to our advantage, as well."

Colbosh growled out something with a series of tongue clicks before the droid responded. "Recapturing the *Dawson* with the aid of the crew is the only choice at present, Owner. I do not have enough information about the enemy presence to give you any other alternatives."

Had Colbosh wanted to leave them behind and find his own path off this world? Was that what the conversation had been about? Michelle thought.

"I don't know what just transpired," Frost said. "But I need your help, Colbosh. I can't take the base on my own."

Colbosh had turned, looking past her now at the admiral as he roared out something and beat his chest with one hand. There was hate in those dark orbs he called eyes.

"You are responsible for the death of my owner's people. Justice must be served," Dim said.

The admiral's face was unmoving, as if it had been carved out of stone. Was there any sincerity in his admission? Why had Colbosh spared him in the first place? She thought Colbosh must have had a plan for using the man. Did that mean that there was someone else beyond the admiral who had orchestrated the death of his people?

"I was only doing what I thought was the right thing at the time. Humanity couldn't afford another war with the Artrans. I know that's no excuse for what I did. I regret it now, Colbosh."

Still that stone cold expression on his face. The admiral was lying; Frost was as bad as Dante, perhaps even worse. Colbosh should kill him now. How could she relay her concerns to him? And if she did, how would this affect her survival? If Colbosh killed the man then there would be no escape from this world.

Colbosh beat on his chest again, followed by another string of growls. There was still a lot of rage radiating out from him. The admiral would be lucky if Colbosh let him live again, she thought.

"Owner," Dim said. "In our present circumstance we need the admiral's help. I do suggest we take it. Killing him now will not help us in our quest to avenge your people, Owner."

Colbosh let out another roar.

Dim said, "My owner agrees to spare your life, Admiral, as long as you agree to help him find the ambassador."

"Agreed," Frost said.

What ambassador? Michelle thought. Was he referring to the Artran Ambassador? It sounded like the admiral had been responsible for the execution of the plan and he justified it by the survival of humanity. The man was as cold and cruel as Dante had been.

Only Johnas had had a heart. Both Colbosh and the admiral deserved to die.

"We need weapons," Frost said.

"There are weapons in the next room below the bridge," Dim said. "The body in the next room also needs to be restrained."

Colbosh's eyes never left the admiral's as the man crawled down the small access port. In her opinion they were going to kill each other when the timing was convenient; she only hoped it wouldn't happen during their escape.

The canopy was closing back around her. There were grinding and crunching noises as the legs pulled free from the cliff's surface and began ascending to the top backwards. If she had to choose a side to help, it would have to be Colbosh's. She didn't trust the admiral; there was too much of his brother in him for her to trust him.

CHAPTER NINE

The fire raged around them, but the machine maneuvered through the flames unharmed. The smoke was so dense Colbosh couldn't see anything through the canopy. His droid remained in control of the machine and had no problem navigating it back to the pirate base. The fire had spread back to the base, which was creating the kind of panic they needed to sneak in. Up above the stone structure was a landing platform where several shuttles were parked. Pirates were already rushing toward them as they approached. They didn't have much time to act, Colbosh thought.

The chamber down below the bridge had been stocked with several weapons. There were several AR-517s, two pistols, and a badly kept shotgun. The admiral had taken one of the AR-517s and a pistol. Colbosh had taken the other, leaving a pistol and the shotgun for Michelle. Michelle wouldn't be any good to them in the base, but they could use her to defend a position. They hoped to get control of a shuttle early then Michelle could defend it. Due to the position of the shuttles, Dim could remain in control of the machine and help protect the shuttles, as well.

"Owner," Dim said. The connection he had with his droid was no longer there, a product of the damage his droid had taken out in the jungle. "One of the shuttles is starting to leave the platform. What are your orders?"

The shuttle had to be stopped. The more pirates they killed down here the less they'd have to face in space. He growled out the order to destroy the shuttle. In obedience to his command, his droid let loose a beam of white light from the belly of the machine. Despite the smoke, Colbosh could see well enough to watch the beam cut instantly through the aft hull of the shuttle and plummet back down to the landing pad. Fire erupted from the wreck as it smashed into another shuttle, and the pirates that had been boarding it scattered in all directions. That left three more shuttles on the platform.

"I can decrease the intensity of the fire, Owner, so it will not damage the shuttles if you wish to use it against the targets."

"That'll make our jobs a lot easier," Frost said, standing next to Michelle with his AR-517 slung over his shoulder.

Colbosh clicked his tongue in the roof of his mouth. It was frustrating having to communicate with his droid like this. It slowed down everything, including getting tactical information he needed about the area.

Fire burst forth from the belly of the machine as his droid brought it right to the edge of the landing platform. Some of the pirates that had been standing on the platform trying to get on a shuttle turned and started firing at them. The bullets ricocheted harmlessly off the armor of the machine. None of the pirates had time to take cover when the flames reached them. It was intense, and at first he couldn't see anything, but as his eyes adjusted to it, he saw several of the pirates incinerate in the flames. Others that hadn't caught the full force of the blast were rolling on the ground, trying to put the flames out.

"My sensors detect a few hostiles remaining in the shuttles, but all threats have been removed from the platform. Opening canopy."

The smoke filled Colbosh's lungs instantly and made him cough. There hadn't been any respirators or any kind of survival gear on board the machine. Once they took over a shuttle, though, especially one that came from the *Dawson*, they would find masks and other gear they could use.

Frost was the first out, crawling along the armored body of the machine and stepping off onto the platform. When he touched down, he took his rifle from his shoulder and began scanning the perimeter. Colbosh followed after him and then Michelle came in behind. Most of the bodies were still burning, but there was no movement anywhere. All was still, except for the crunching sounds of the jungle around them being torn apart.

He took the lead, heading toward the first shuttle closest to them. The door was still open and there were burning bodies all the way into the interior. Peeking inside all he found was more burning bodies and an interior that appeared to have been melted. Displays had burst under the intensity of the heat and control panels had turned to goo.

This shuttle was definitely out of commission. He would have searched it for a respirator, but the fire had caused so much damage there was little chance that equipment would have survived. The two shuttles past this should have fared much better, since they were farther from the blast. He crept along the left side of the shuttle and motioned for Frost to go to the right. Michelle had fallen in step behind him. When he peered around the side, he heard a gunshot. A bullet ricocheted off the armor of the shuttle near him.

There were several more shots, some of which had sounded like they had come from Frost. When he peered around again he found the pirate that had been shooting at him dead and lying face down in the entrance of the shuttle.

Frost charged up to the door, unimpeded by any more threats. Once Frost was in position, Colbosh ran in behind him and took up position on the opposite side of the door. There was some argument going on inside of the shuttle that he couldn't make out. When he peered inside he saw a pirate peering from around the side of the cockpit wall. The pirate didn't have a chance to scream when Colbosh's bullet went through his head. He charged forward and caught the other pirate, who had been so shocked that he was simply sitting on the floor, just staring at his dead comrade. Colbosh put a bullet in his chest.

"Owner," his droid said from a small communication device he had picked up in the machine. It was pinned to the collar of his armored jumpsuit. "More pirates are attempting to come onto the roof."

The flame weapon had worked well before, so he ordered his droid to use it again. That would buy them some more time to get control of the other shuttle.

"Found them," Frost said with several deep coughs. The man was in a compartment above the seats, pulling out several masks with a canister attached to them. There were ten or fifteen in all, so there would be enough for them plus some of the surviving crew, if any were still alive by the time they reached them.

Frost tossed him one of the masks but when Colbosh placed it over his head, it didn't fit over his snout. When he had served with the humans during the war, they had made such devices for his race, but not now. He tossed it to the floor with a snarl.

"I'm sorry, Colbosh, but there wasn't one on board. The *Dawson* was built after the war, when your race was no longer needed for the effort."

That was because many of his kind had been sacrificed by human commanders who sent his people in first to enemy traps. There hadn't been many of his kind left after the war, and those that did survive found themselves placed on a human experimental world. Some reward for all the sacrifices his people had made. He coughed again. How long could he withstand this smoke? His lungs were already hurting and he felt light-headed.

"If the last shuttle is from an older ship," Frost began, but Colbosh was no longer listening. He was heading toward the exit of the shuttle. He had only two options; either find something fast or retreat to the machine.

He charged recklessly toward the other shuttle; fortunately for him there had been only one surviving pirate on board and he was in the pilot's chair, banging his fist on the console, unsure what to press to get the thing to fly. Colbosh disposed of the man quickly and tore apart the overhead bins in an attempt to find a respirator. Tons of human ones hit the floor. Desperation began to grow in the back of his mind. How much more time? His coughing had intensified, along with his head spinning.

At the last bin three odd-shaped masks fell from the compartment. He pulled one on, and it fit perfectly. After several deep breaths he was still coughing, but he could breath freely now. Frost found him still on the floor and he offered a hand to him. Colbosh refused it and hauled himself up. There was a satchel slung around the admiral's shoulder; he sat down on the floor and began cramming more of the masks into it.

"We don't have much time. Michelle is prepping the shuttle. We need to get into the base now."

He wished the coughing would stop; it would be an annoyance to him during combat.

"Let's go," Frost urged him.

If he could just kill the human now and leave this world, but the universe had led him to this moment and he had no choice but to help the human. Perhaps the souls of his people had a more fitting end in mind for this man.

"I said let's go."

Colbosh followed after the man as they ran across the platform to the stairwell entrance into the base. Burning bodies lined the steps down where his droid had held the pirates at bay. It was surprising to find no resistance as they entered the main part of the base; what few pirates that were still alive were running about in panic. Some even looked straight at them, but did nothing.

There was gunfire all around, but it wasn't directed at them. Marching further in they came across several dead pirates all killed by gunshots. At first Colbosh thought that perhaps some of the *Dawson*'s crew had gotten free, but instead what they found was a lone human, obviously a pirate due to his ragged clothing, killing anyone he came across.

Humans were such pathetic creatures when faced with uncertain futures. Their minds snapped as this one's had. But before Colbosh could kill the rampaging human, he caught sight of something moving through the smoke. At first his mind couldn't make out the shape, but then the figure emerged, cutting down the rampaging human with a small hand ax.

It was another of his kind standing before him; Colbosh couldn't smell him, but the brand in his arm identified him as a member of the clan orbo. Colbosh didn't want to have to kill another of his kind, but the feuds between clans were something that no one of his race could ignore. Even now he could feel his heart pounding deep within his chest. It was like a madness sweeping over him that he must obey. He charged the other, abandoning his weapon and drawing the knife from his boot.

The other Nomad had seen him coming, but hadn't moved. When Colbosh hit him, he felt both of their bodies give way, and they went tumbling over each other.

Frost had lost sight of Colbosh. The smoke was so thick that sight was reduced to just a foot or two in front of him. He had a communication device pinned to his shirt, and with Dim's guidance he had managed to navigate to the stairwell leading down to the prison chambers. To his delight several crew members being led by a group of Marines had intercepted him.

There was recognition amongst just about everyone in the group, and he lowered his weapon. "I'm Admiral Frost. Who's in charge?"

A short woman in Marine fatigues and a shaved head approached him from the group. "I'm Colonel Rosa of the third fleet division," she said with a salute.

He returned it. "How many survivors do you have?"

"Fifteen Marines and twenty crew men, sir. There are more survivors on board the *Dawson*."

"I'm aware of that, Colonel."

"Where's the rescue party?" someone said from the crowd.

He didn't answer. Instead he handed the bag of masks to the colonel and she began distributing them to the survivors. Now was the time to lead, and he would lead these people to safety. To hell with what happened to Colbosh; it saved Frost from having to deal with him later.

"Follow me," he ordered the survivors. They all stayed packed together; each person had a hand on another person as they navigated through the smoke.

The pirates they encountered they killed on contact. There was no organized resistance against them as they made it to the stairwell leading up to the shuttles.

At one point he thought he caught a glimpse of Colbosh, but the smoke was thick and the fire was spreading to everything in the structure. Dim indicated that his owner was no longer on his sensors and he couldn't raise him on the communicator. That was fine with Frost. Michelle had reported getting both shuttles prepped and was ready to go as soon as they arrived.

He was the last survivor up the stairwell along with a Marine. He wanted to make sure no one was left behind, no human, at least. At the top of the stairs and on the platform he saw several Marines carrying the unconscious body of Dante and another of his lackeys toward the shuttles. Colonel Rosa was standing out supervising everyone as crew men filed in.

He should've killed Dante on board the machine, he thought, but then the capture of his brother would increase moral in the fleet. And it would definitely divert any attention that had been drawn toward him about the accident on Chevron Five. Not that anyone had a clue other than Colbosh, or at least that he knew of. He should've tried to get more information out of the alien, especially how he had uncovered Frost's involvement in the affair. As a captain had told him once when he was just a junior officer, it was all damage control from here.

The colonel saluted him as he stepped into line to board the shuttle nearest the stairwell.

"Admiral, the pirate Dante has been secured. As soon as everyone is aboard we'll lift off. If you plan on retaking the *Dawson*, we're going to need more weapons."

"Sorry, Colonel, we're just going to have to make due. We may get lucky and surprise the pirates on the *Dawson* if we act fast."

"The woman pilot reports communication from the ships in orbit to the base, but so far, according to her, they are unaware of the situation.

"Good, let's keep all communications silent. Without leadership, the pirates will be disorganized. Surprise is the only tactical advantage we have. Hopefully it's enough," Frost said.

"Fortune favors the foolish, Admiral."

"Let's hope you're right, Colonel."

"Sir." A Marine came up beside the colonel and saluted. "We may have a problem with the woman pilot."

"Explain?" the colonel said.

"Sir, she refuses to leave without someone named Colbosh."

"I will deal with this, Colonel," Frost said. "Find me someone who can pilot this ship while I talk to her. If she continues to refuse I may need your services in removing her."

"Understood," Colonel Rosa said.

He should've known that Michelle would be a problem. Now he wished he hadn't given her weapons. How much did she know about him? Had Colbosh confided in her? He would have to dispose of her, as well.

Michelle had the shotgun propped against the pilot's chair when he entered into the cockpit, and the pistol was resting in her lap. She looked back at him as he approached.

"Where's Colbosh?"

Her right hand rested on the pistol.

"I lost sight of him in the base," Frost said. "There were a lot of stray firefights going on down there. It's possible he was hit by one, or any number of things."

"Don't lie to me. I'm not stupid, you know. What did you do to him?"

"I admit that I wanted Colbosh dead because he tried to kill me, but I swear to you that I didn't do anything to him."

"Just shut it. We're not going anywhere. You're just like Dante. I know what you did, Admiral."

There was the confirmation he needed. She knew and therefore she had to perish along with the alien. She was beautiful except for her ear, which was visible because her hair was pulled back into a tail. He had to act; if he rushed her he could tie her hands up and prevent her from grabbing the gun completely. With a few shouts the Marines would be in to help.

He rushed her just as he had planned, but she managed to get one hand around the pistol when his hands gripped hers. He knew he was taking a risk as he screamed out for help. She was strong and his muscles were weak from climbing the cliff. It didn't take long for her to overpower him and break the weapon away from his grasp, but by the time she aimed it at him armed Marines had rushed in. One of them smashed his rifle butt into the side of her head and she collapsed to the floor.

"You all, right, Admiral?" the colonel said.

"I'm fine; did you find me a pilot?"

"This is Lieutenant Saul," she said, ushering a young man into the room. "He's a pilot on the *Dawson.*

"Excellent. If the other shuttle is ready, let's get out of here," Frost said.

Saul took a seat in the pilot's chair. He pressed several buttons and the shuttle began to lift from the ground. Out the window the other shuttle was lifting off, as well.

For some reason Saul looked to the right of the cockpit window. There was an expression on Saul's face Frost couldn't quite comprehend until he saw the giant leg of the spider-like machine crashing down around him. He fell to the floor under the impact and the lights went off for a few seconds before cycling back on.

"What the hell happened?" the colonel said, on the floor with him.

Why the hell had he forgotten about the droid? Frost thought.

At some point Colbosh's mask had been knocked from his face. His lungs were burning, the coughs had returned with a vengeance, and the worst part about it was that he was losing to this other Nomad. Blood was pouring from his nose and several of his teeth were missing. The rest of his body was completely exhausted, an obvious result of his abuse on the cliffs. Even now he was on his back, trying to keep the sharp edge of the enemy's ax away from his face.

The blade struck the ground next to his head, which gave him the opportunity to trap the other's arm.

His body may have been exhausted, but his muscles remembered moves he had trained his whole life for, moves his clansmen had drilled into him since he was a youngling trying to survive in the human mines.

With the other Nomad's arm trapped, Colbosh used his left leg to wrap around the other's face. The enemy struggled against his trap, but Colbosh didn't provide him any time. With a quick thrust of his hip he pulled the other down, but a cramp in his leg caused the enemy to break free from his grip. Another burst of coughing rolled him to his side. His vision was starting to black out. It wouldn't be long before he lost consciousness all together.

"I don't want to fight," the other Nomad said in human tongue.

How could he speak English? His kind was incapable of generating their speech patterns. But there had been scars on the other's neck; had he been an experiment of some kind? An experiment by the humans - like Colbosh had been.

"I know our code makes us natural enemies, but I'm not like the other of my clansmen that attacked you in the jungle."

Colbosh could hear the words, but the adrenaline was pulsing through his veins. All he could see in his mind's eye was tearing the throat from his enemy and letting the blood spill over him.

After another coughing fit he rushed him, and this time the other sidestepped him and he collapsed into a burning debris pile. His jumpsuit protected him as he rolled through it, but a large support beam collapsed on his back, pinning him to the floor.

All the air rushed from his lungs and he couldn't get any more clean air. Darkness filled his vision. His quest was over, he thought as he blacked out.

Frost was back on his feet. The colonel looked stunned by the turn of events, but still capable of carrying out his orders if he gave them to her. The young man Saul still had his head covered. What could he say to the droid? What if he sent the Marines to take out the droid? Then it would take them time to figure out how to move the machine.

He reached down for the communicator on his shirt. "Dim?" That's how he had heard Michelle refer to the machine.

"Your shuttle is the only means for my owner to escape this planet. You cannot leave until he arrives."

"Dim, the last report I got from Michelle was that you had lost contact with your owner. Has something changed?"

"No. Standard protocol states that if communication has been lost then I must wait an hour to see if communications or some kind of contact has been restored."

"Is he kidding?" the colonel said, standing beside him.

"I'm afraid not," he said. "Dim, we don't have an hour. If we're going to get out of this system we need to leave now."

"My owner needs your shuttle to escape. I will not let you leave until he arrives."

"Could we take him out?" the colonel said.

"Prepare your men; it looks like we may not have a choice."

The colonel disappeared into the main hold. Saul looked up at Frost from the control board.

"Sir," Saul said. "The other shuttle pilot is requesting orders."

"Have him stay low and nearby, we may need to abandon this shuttle. Strike that, Lieutenant. Have that shuttle land. Colonel, have your people start boarding the other shuttle. We don't have time to waste."

"Understood, sir," the colonel said with a salute.

Colbosh couldn't see but he could feel himself being pulled by the arms. His torso hurt and his lungs burned like someone had stuck coals in them. But the smoke was no longer entering his lungs and for the first time he realized that his mask had been replaced on his face. Through the smoke he could make out an outline of the other Nomad dragging him along the floor. For some reason he had freed Colbosh from the beam that had collapsed on him during their fight. If it would've been him, he would have left his enemy to die.

After being dragged several more feet he felt the other Nomad stop, then collapse to the floor. His own body felt weak and unresponsive but he managed to crawl on his knees to the side of the other Nomad. His chest was still heaving up and down, but his eyes were closed tight in unconsciousness. The thought of why this enemy had saved him played out in Colbosh's mind and he couldn't find an explanation for it. His clan was enemies of this one's; this Nomad should've left him for dead.

"Owner, are you there?" his droid said through the communicator still buttoned to his ruined jumpsuit. The fire had eaten most of it away, except for the underlining that had protected him from the heat. The bio-impact layer and the armored weave were gone, patchy in some areas but not enough to protect him in a combat situation.

With a cough he called back to his droid.

"Owner, there is a significant buildup of energy in the base. It will reach a critical point in about five minutes. I suggest you hurry to the roof. Admiral Frost and Michelle have already left; I did manage to secure one of the shuttles for you."

He staggered to his feet, feeling sore all over his body. There was no time to delay; he had to make a run for the shuttle. But what should he do about his enemy? He had saved Colbosh's life for some reason. He would learn why. Kneeling, he lifted the other up onto his shoulder. The extra weight would slow him down.

"Hurry, Owner, three minutes to critical," his droid said over the communicator again. He was near the top of the stairwell; from deep down below him he heard explosions.

"I've cleared the landing pad and have the systems up and running aboard the shuttle. I do suggest you hurry, Owner, only two minutes and thirty-five seconds remaining."

Another explosion from down below tumbled him out of the doorway just as a ball of flame shot out from behind him. Up ahead his droid had the loading ramp down and he rushed toward it. Around him sections of the roof began to collapse as support beams gave way. Large stones once held in place by beams began to crash back to the earth. Nature was reclaiming its own, as it always did, unyielding to anyone or anything.

One of the large stones gave way beneath his foot as he stepped onto the ramp. Fire licked up at his heels as his droid floated the ship away. Once the door was shut the shuttle lifted rapidly toward the sky.

"Ten seconds to critical," his droid said. The force of the takeoff had pinned him against the ramp door; he couldn't move anything at the moment.

There was a thud from behind him and he was propelled forward into some of the seats along with the unconscious enemy Nomad. It felt like the shuttle was taking a nose dive for the surface, but then it straightened out and was once again heading for space.

Frost took the charge on the bridge of the *Dawson* with the colonel at his side and several Marines. So far they had surprised any resistance on board the ship. Without leadership, the pirates were just as he had thought: a pack of wild dogs without a leader to guide them.

A couple of pirates had been stationed on the bridge; they had taken defensive positions and started firing at Frost and his crew as they came through the door. A bullet had hit his arm, but with his adrenaline pumping he had stood his ground and killed the pirate closest to the command chair.

Within seconds all of the pirates were down, four in all, but unfortunately one of his Marines was down, too. Rosa was by the man, but blood was jetting from a wound to his throat.

"Get him to the med bay," the colonel said.

Two Marines lifted the fallen soldier while a third held gauze pads from a med pack to the wound. As they left, the former crew of the *Dawson* filled in and began taking positions.

Saul took the helm; others that Frost didn't recognize took their posts. A lot of the *Dawson*'s crew had been secured on board the ship. Dante had only taken down enough to give his men some sport; those that had been killed were mostly high-ranking officers.

"All systems are go," he hears from the officers at their stations. Through the parasteel window in the front of the ship, pirate ships were beginning to maneuver toward them. Marching to the tactical station, a large table with displays set up in the center of the bridge, Frost took in the situation. There were five pirate ships in this area of space with them, all of which had apparently figured out what was happening and closing in to attack position.

The colonel came up beside him as Saul called out for orders from the helm. "Break orbit," Frost said.

"What about the shuttle leaving the planet's surface?" the colonel pointed out to him.

He hadn't seen it when he was looking earlier; was it the other shuttle they had left on the rooftop? Was it just the droid or had his owner survived somehow?

A male officer from another station reported a distress call from the shuttle. It was the droid, along with his owner and another survivor.

"Helm, delay my order. Colonel, go and greet our guests. Have them detained, but beware, if the alien is armed, he will be dangerous." If it had just been the droid and his owner, Frost would've been able to leave them behind, but if there was another survivor it would raise suspicion on his part. He would have to deal with the alien in another way.

On the display the hostile ships outlined in red were well within the *Dawson*'s firing range. The problem, however, was that the pirates had managed to lock out the weapons control along with several other key systems. The only thing they had available to them at the moment was propulsion.

"Helm, as soon as that shuttle touches the landing bay, get us the hell out of here."

If only they could get their weapons back online. "Firing control, what's our status?" Frost said.

The young male technician at the station looked at him as if he had heard a bad joke. "Working on it, sir."

None of this would've been possible if that traitor Price had been executed on board his station instead of being sent back to Earth for disposal. He could try and get the codes out of Dante, but that would take too much time, Frost thought.

"Breaking orbit," Saul said.

The ship moved beneath his feet, turning and pivoting, breaking free from the gravitational pull of the planet beneath him. On the tactical display the nearest pirate ships were firing grappling hooks at them. They intended to pin him in place, but they were not going to capture him again.

"Helm, evasive maneuvers, put all power to the engines." The first grappling hook fired missed the ship entirely, another glanced off the *Dawson*'s armor, but two others penetrated the outer armor and were holding. The *Dawson* was a powerful ship; it would take more than just those two ships to hold it in place. If a third or fourth caught hold, they would be in trouble.

The pirate ships that had failed were coming about to try again. What were his options? If he had weapons he could've destroyed all of those ships by now, but that wasn't the case. There was only one option left to him.

Scrolling through the display, he highlighted one of the pirate ships that had hooked them. It was in a key position for them to ram it, but he wanted to know what kind of ship it was. As it turned out it was a light freighter of older design. The armor had been modified but it was nowhere as tough as the *Dawson*'s hull.

"Helm, ram the starboard pirate ship, full thrust."

There was a moment of hesitation from the helmsman before he responded. "Yes, sir."

On impact Frost had to hold on to the bars around the table, but after the initial jolt the *Dawson* pushed on through the pirate freighter. From the window he watched the freighter disintegrate under their bulk. Automated systems began sending him damage reports on the *Dawson*. So far the front armor had taken minor damage.

"Sir, we've broken the grapples," the helmsman reported.

The display indicated that to be accurate; apparently some of the wreckage from the freighter had torn the other grapple loose, as well. But something else was happening; the other pirate ships were slowing down. They were letting them go.

"Helm, how long before we can jump from this system?" Frost said.

He could've looked up the information for himself, but it was good to keep the crew involved sometimes.

"Five hours. Where to?" The helmsman said.

In all the excitement he didn't have a clue where he was, but after a few inquires on the tactical display he was able to plot them a course back from wild space and near a C.E.F. outpost. That left only one thing to do, how to deal with the alien and his companions.

CHAPTER TEN

Wild space

After they had jumped from the system, with no more pursuit from the pirates, Frost had found the captain's ready room. There was a small personal bathroom with a shower that he used. His clothes were ruined, so he tried on some of the captain's spare uniforms, which fit almost perfectly. The sleeves were a little short, but they would just have to do.

At some point during the trip communications had been restored. He was updated to the present circumstances, but his technicians still had not found a way to free the lock on the weapons control. Once they reached C.E.F. space, they were heading straight for the nearest star base. There shouldn't be any need for the weapons, but he would feel better if they were online.

The door to the ready room swished open. Colonel Rosa marched in and saluted him. "Reporting as ordered."

"Please, have a seat, Colonel."

She had cleaned her face but not her clothing. She had a beautiful face, very round and smooth, except for the black bags under her eyes. It was obvious as she took a seat and from the slump in her posture that she was tired.

Come to think about it, how long had it been since he had had any real sleep? His body felt like it was still coming off an adrenaline rush. How long before he couldn't function anymore? After the meeting with her he would go down to medical and find something to help him sleep.

"Colonel, I would like to update you about events. It appears that the Artran council has come forward to the C.E.F. and declared that Ambassador Lor'ta has been responsible for the string of attacks on us."

"What do they propose to do about it?"

"I was getting to that," Frost said, collapsing his hands on the table in front of him. "A fleet comprised of our forces and the Artrans is in route to World 2167, the supposed stronghold of the ambassador. It's the belief of the council that if they are to eliminate the ambassador, whatever force he's controlling will stop."

"Why are you telling me all of this, sir?"

She was smart, he thought. "I trust you, Colonel, as I hope you trust me."

"With my life, Admiral."

He couldn't help but smile. "There's a situation I need you to handle for me."

"Name it, sir."

"The alien and his companions we've got in the holding cells. What no one knows right now is that I was kidnapped by force from my flagship during the confrontation with the wraiths. The alien blames all responsibility on me for the accident on Chevron Five. I had nothing to do with it."

"What are you asking of me, Admiral?"

"I would like for them to disappear, all of them." He slumped back in his chair, his arms now resting on the armrests.

The colonel's brown eyes never left his as she spoke. "I understand, sir; I will deal with it personally."

"Thank you, Colonel. I will make sure you and your command are highly commended when we get home."

She saluted one more time and left the room. Loyalty was a wonderful thing. It had to be one of the C.E.F.'s greatest strengths. It's what held the fleets together during the war.

Now that the matter of the alien was taken care of, it was time to take care of his needs. He hoped the med bay was well supplied.

Colbosh sat in a cell by himself; he was still coughing and his sense of smell was completely out of whack. His connection with his droid was still impaired and he had no clue to the state of the others. The only thing that was apparent was that the *Dawson* had escaped from the pirates and was now on its way back to C.E.F.-controlled space.

A rattling at his cell door brought him out of his thoughts. Two armed Marines, now in full tactical gear, stood there motioning for him to step out. They were taking him to be interrogated or perhaps Frost was going to have him eliminated. That was the most logical outcome.

They cuffed his arms and escorted him at gunpoint to a cargo hold. Once inside he knew what Frost's plan was for them. The other Nomad was standing near a pile of dead pirate bodies. Michelle and Devin were beside him, looking at Colbosh. They were going to be executed. He walked between Michelle and the other Nomad. He was speaking to the Marines.

"I need to speak to your commanding officer," the other Nomad said. "My name is Suntol; I have information about the Artrans."

The alien had called himself Suntol; Colbosh would remember it, like the names of all his clansmen that had perished at Chevron Five.

A short female with colonel's bars on her uniform entered the cargo bay with two more Marines. They lined up with the others, their weapons still down at their sides, but the tension was growing. All the Marines had their hands on the grips, ready to go at any notice.

"Why am I here?" Devin said, running his fingers through his hair. His eyes were wide with fright. Michelle was trying to calm him down, but the Marines ordered her to back away from him.

Would his avenging clansmen be able to get him out of this? Death kept knocking at his door and sooner or later it would find a way in.

"Colonel," Suntol said with a cough. "I need to speak with you; I have information vital to the C.E.F."

The colonel said nothing as she pulled her pistol from its holster. "Take aim."

The Marines had their weapons lined up on each one of them. Frost had won; the humans had won, Colbosh thought.

"Please, I beg you," Suntol said. "I know that Ambassador Lor'ta has used a weapon of the Ancients' against the humans. I know where the world is, I can help you stop him."

There was no emotion in the colonel's face. If it was true that Suntol knew about the ambassador, then it was possible he could get him close to him. His avenging clansmen had led this survivor to his path to help Colbosh bring justice to the galaxy. So why was he know facing a firing squad?

The man called Devin had fallen to his knees weeping and sobbing out of control. He was pleading for his life. The colonel should've ordered her men to fire by now, but instead she stepped up to Devin and slammed the butt of her pistol into his temple. Devin clumped to the floor, unconscious.

"Hold your position," she said and left the room.

The marines held their rifles on them and they wouldn't move until given orders otherwise. If any of them moved or tried to do anything, they would be shot.

The colonel didn't come back; instead one of the Marines escorted Suntol from the cargo bay. It felt like hours they were gone. Devin had regained consciousness and was behaving himself. Michelle stood motionless with hate radiating off her. Some of it was focused toward Colbosh, but most of it was directed at the Marines watching them.

The cargo bay doors opened. Frost and the colonel escorted Suntol back into the room. Suntol walked directly in front of Colbosh and he no longer had restraints on.

"If we follow tradition," Suntol said, "we would have to kill each other. I don't have this hate toward you, Colbosh."

Suntol might not hate him, but being this close to his enemy made Colbosh's heart race. Just like before, thoughts of feeling the other's blood running over his hands poured through his mind. "The old ways are not easy to ignore."

"I understand. What I'm asking is for us to put aside our clans' oath and work together as quest brothers. We have a common enemy that presents a threat to all of us.

His fate, he guessed, probably rested on his next words. What Suntol had said made sense; he just had to keep his hate in check. "I will suspend the old ways until our common foe is destroyed," he said in his native tongue.

Suntol moved toward one of the Marines and asked for a blade. The soldier obliged him and Suntol cut his palm open and then passed Colbosh the blade. There was intense pain at first as he slid the steel across his palm, but then it was gone. There was just a dull ache in his hand as he pressed his palm into Suntol's chest.

Suntol did the same until their black blood ran down their chests. It was an old ritual, quite common during the war and in the mines, when feuding clans competed against each other.

"We're now quest brothers," Suntol said.

The admiral said nothing, but there was a look in his eyes as if his prey had gotten away. Whatever Suntol had told him; it was convincing enough to keep them alive, for now anyway

CHAPTER ELEVEN

Colbosh found himself buckled into the seat in an assault pod. Marines were all around him, in full tactical gear, including the colonel. His droid had been placed in a storage compartment above his head; some of the *Dawson*'s technicians had tried to repair his link with it, but to no avail. It would take someone more skilled than them. It didn't really matter. This was a one-way trip into hell anyway. It was likely that none of them would survive this.

If Suntol was right about the wraiths, then they wouldn't bother the assault pods with him in it. Suntol was unsure why the wraiths wouldn't harm his race; it didn't make any sense to him, either. His clansmen had brought him to this point, however, and no matter what happened next he truly believed he would get his chance to bring justice to his people.

Frost spoke over the assault pod's intercom. "We're nearing the planet, and our fleets are engaged with several wraith ships. It looks like our forces are holding strong. We now have weapons control and once we drop you off, we're going to form up with the fleet and do what damage we can."

There was a cry from every Marine around him. He never understood what they said, but it had obvious meaning, considering how much time he had spent in the presences of Marines. They were ready to face death.

"Godspeed, Marines, and I'll see you when the smoke clears."

The soldiers cried out again. His people had a way of pumping themselves up for battle, as well, but at the moment he didn't care to demonstrate it. There was only one thought on his mind and that was the death of the ambassador.

The human armor he had put on didn't fit quite right and it itched around his shoulder blades. He wanted his old armor back, but that was impossible. He would have to go back to Earth to acquire a duplicate. None of that mattered now.

The light in the pod went from green to red. After a second's delay, the pod dropped at incredible speed. The g-forces pinned him to his seat. Within a few minutes the pod came to a crashing stop that jarred his whole body. The door popped open and a fine cloud of dust rolled in. The sky was gray, along with the sandy dirt that covered the ground. There were some ruins in the distance but he couldn't make out any details, especially as the marines began unbuckling and pulling their weapons down.

"Thirty seconds," the colonel said.

Colbosh unbuckled himself and released his droid from the hold. His shotgun and an AR-517 acquired from the *Dawson* armory was in the hold, as well. He placed the shotgun around his shoulder and kept the AR-517 in his hands.

"Let's go, Marines," the colonel said, leading the troops down the ramp.

He fell in about halfway. So far Suntol had been right. The wraiths hadn't attacked the pods because they had been on board, but now that they were on the ground, the wraiths, as the humans called them, could pick them off easily.

"Owner, the other drop pod is about half a kilometer to the north. So far my sensors have detected an Artran mobile unit on an intercept course to the other squad."

"How far is our primary objective?" he said in a series of growls.

"The temple indicated by Suntol is three point four kilometers from here. Once there, based on current measurements, it's a total of six point one kilometers into the main temple."

"Let's move it," the colonel said. "Our other force is under fire."

Streaks of fire could be seen ripping through the air as they neared the battle. Fortunately for them, there was plenty of cover from large stones that had fallen from the ruins as they approached. The tank that had been accompanying the Artran force was in smoking ruins up ahead from thermal grenades that had essentially eaten a hole through the side of it.

The colonel was giving out directions for her men as Colbosh took up a position in an old stairwell with plenty of cover. The scope on this model AR-517 wasn't as efficient as ones he had used before, but it would do. His droid called out places for him to look and he found his first target.

An Artran soldier in full tactical gear was cowering behind a stone wall preparing to toss grenades. His shot went straight through the Artran's head, despite the helmet. The *Dawson* had a great supply of military-grade armor-piercing rounds on board. His droid called out another location and he found two Artrans trying to flank some of the Marines. One of his bullets went through the head of the lead Artran, but his other shot missed. It didn't take long for the Marines to run down the survivor and kill him.

"Owner, skimmers and more mobile units are en route to this location. I have already informed Colonel Rosa. She wants all of her troops to move double time toward the entry point."

Why only ground troops to stop them, he wondered. Could it be that all of the ambassador's attention was focused on the space battle and that he was relying on his ground forces to deal with them? It certainly couldn't be the fact that he and Suntol were here. They were protected for some reason, but the humans wouldn't be.

"Suntol reports his team has arrived at the entry point, so far no resistance."

Why was it so easy so far? Hadn't the ambassador expected that assault pods would've made it to the ground? According to Suntol, the wraiths gave the ambassador a slight precognitive ability. He could see a few moments into the future through the wraiths, which gave him an incredible advantage over any opponent. That's why none of this felt right.

By the time he reached the entry point, some of the Artran ground forces had caught up with them. He followed the last of the Marines providing cover fire into the tunnels. A demolitionist was already placing explosives in the stairwell. The Marines still used the old string-type explosives because they were harder to detect than the newer ones the Artrans favored. It was always amazing to him that the Artrans claimed themselves to be so superior to the humans, yet they modeled just about all their weapons off the humans.

"Still no resistance up ahead," Dim said. Was it possible they were marching to their deaths or had the wraiths' precognitive ability failed the ambassador? Perhaps it had given him a blind side. That was all Colbosh could hope for.

The tunnels were long and tall, but not very wide; two Marines could go through side by side, but that was the extent of the room they had. There was a maze of tunnels down here. If Suntol hadn't given them a map it would be real easy to get lost. "Suntol reports exit point is clear. Colonel Rosa has ordered her men in."

He wasn't too far behind the main group and there were still Marines behind him, some of which were setting up traps along the way. Suntol was waiting for him at the top of the stairs. The stairway led out of a large stone box; its lid had been removed.

Throughout the room there were more stone boxes with ornate statues carved into them, followed by statues such he had seen on the tech world colony. This was an Ancient's world for sure.

"This is only one of the smaller burial chambers," Suntol said. "You should see the lower level. There are statues down there that stretch to the roof, not of Ancients but of us, Colbosh, and the statues speak. It's there that the ambassador discovered the orbs, or what the humans call wraiths."

"Where is the ambassador?" Colbosh said.

"His usual habit was to pace the main throne room."

"Then that's where we must go."

"Are you in such a hurry to join your clansmen, Colbosh?" Suntol said.

"Justice must be served."

"And it will, in its own time."

Dim said, "Colonel Rosa reports that the corridor is clear."

"Seems too easy, doesn't it, Colbosh? Suntol said. The ambassador knows we're here and none of us are safe. The wraiths may not hurt us directly, but the ambassador can use them to cause damage to things around us. If we manage to kill him, then it will truly be our clansmen guiding our hand."

As they proceeded through the halls and corridors, the place was as empty as the tombs they had left. The king's chamber was a large room with stone columns circled all around it; up above was a view of the darkening sky. The ambassador stood stone still in the middle of the room. His head was down and his eyes were closed. Two of the wraiths floated around him, but didn't react to Colbosh and Suntol as the Marines took positions around the stone columns.

Suntol had advised the colonel not to place her men this way, but military thinking was so strict sometimes. When she gave the order to fire on the wraiths protecting the ambassador, they absorbed every single shot fired. For the first time the ambassador raised his head slightly, but his eyes remained closed.

Colonel Rosa gave the order to free fire, but even then the wraiths absorbed everything; that's when the wraiths broke free and began annihilating the Marines one by one.

During the carnage Suntol had pulled his ax from his belt and charged headlong into the ambassador, who simply sidestepped him with his eyes still closed.

Rosa was ordering her men to retreat as Colbosh leveled his weapon next to a stone column himself and fired several bursts at the ambassador. As before, the wraiths intercepted his bullets except one of the wraiths broke off its attack from the Marines and passed by him, so close that the light it gave off temporarily blinded him. It didn't injure him; it simply destroyed the barrel portion of his weapon.

"Owner, do you wish for me to engage?"

Dim was floating directly behind him as his eyesight returned. For the life of him he wished that killing the ambassador would've been simpler, but the way the battle was proceeding, all hope of survival was vanishing.

"Help the Marines escape," he said through a series of growls and clicks of his tongue.

"As you wish, Owner." With that, his droid floated away, trailing after the surviving soldiers that had fled out into the corridor. One of the wraiths pursued them. They were as good as dead, he thought.

Suntol had tried to reengage the ambassador, but as before the ambassador simply sidestepped every attack. It was time for Colbosh to join in; perhaps he and Suntol together could take whatever the ambassador had become. He hoped his avenging ancestors guided his hand in the killing blow. With a howl he pulled the blade from his boot and rushed the ambassador.

Admiral Frost stood over the tactical display on the bridge of the C.E.F. Dawson. The collation fleet was suffering badly. Out of the two hundred ships engaged with three wraith ships, fifty ships had been destroyed so far and numerous were taking damage from the wraiths. Even the *Dawson* had come under attack by several wraiths, just after they had made their pass over the planet. Two wraiths had penetrated the lower hull, only doing minor damage. The *Dawson* was fast, but not fast enough to escape a swarm of wraiths approaching.

Whatever weapons he ordered fired at them did nothing; it seemed as if they didn't exist in real space. No intelligence he had received from the fleet revealed any way to stop them, nor did it include any insight as to their existence. So how in the hell were they to be stopped, he thought, slamming his fist into the display. The only thing the brains on both sides could come up with was to destroy the ships that carried the wraiths. The ships had to be the power source.

According to his tactical readouts there was no power emitting from the wraith ships. They registered only as cold and lifeless as space. And the fleet had inflicted massive damage to two of the wraith ships, including the one nearest the planet. That ship was being forced into the planet's atmosphere from the massive firepower being directed its way. Was it doing any good?

The tactical display blinked red as the swarm of wraiths reached his ship. What orders could he issue? They were already undertaking evasive maneuvers when they fled from the planet, heading to engage the nearest wraith ship which was closest to the planet. The armor wouldn't stop the things.

"Brace for impact." It was the only thing he could think of to say, even though he knew there would be no impact like a missile or a mine.

The ship shuddered around him and the lights went out, followed by the displays. They cut back on in a moment, but not the lights. The red emergency light lit the bridge in an eerie glow. He could hear the bridge crew shouting around him. Damage reports were coming in from all over the ship. His tactical display never came back online.

"Hull breeches on deck six and seven," one person reported.

"Computers offline," another said.

It was the same all over the bridge. The *Dawson* was a dead ship. Frost hadn't wanted to sacrifice her in this way, but there was a chance that Colbosh and the other alien would succeed. None of the other ships had managed to get a ground force to the planet. The wraiths had destroyed them in space. As the other Nomad had told him, they wouldn't harm him. It had been true; they had made it to the ground. After that he didn't know what had happened.

"What are your orders?" the helmsman asked over the reports of others.

"Abandon ship," Frost said.

After the ordeal in the cargo bay, Michelle found herself back in a cell by herself. All the doors were closed and she couldn't see anything other than the four walls around her. There was a toilet in the room, a sink that pulled out of the wall, and the bench/cot she was sitting on.

Everything had spiraled out of control since she met up with Colbosh again. In a way she wished she hadn't had even crossed his path again. That would've meant he would've died back on the Zi-tec world. She wouldn't have known anything about his betrayal of her and she would've mourned his death with honor; now she didn't know what to think.

One minute she wanted the alien dead and the next she found herself helping him again. Why were her emotions so torn on this? The only thing she knew for certain was that Dante was going to get his justice. She had wished that his body had been laid upon the pile of his followers and ejected into space. That was what he deserved, after all.

The lights went out in the cell as she felt the ship tilt to her right for a second. The lights never came back on in her cell, but she could hear people talking outside of her cell. It wasn't clear but it sounded like the voices were saying something about hull breech.

Whatever this Artran ambassador was wielding was immensely powerful. She had never seen a wraith or whatever they were calling those orbs. There was a clicking noise at her door, along with more talking.

"Get her out of there," someone said on the other side.

The door opened and a young male officer stood in front of the bars, illuminated by a red glow from the emergency lighting. The cell had two doors, a barred cage door on the inside and a large metal outer door.

The young officer had a pair of restraints in hand. "Move to the bars and turn around," he said.

"What's happening?"

"No questions. Turn around."

Before she turned around, two other officers stepped up to a cell down the aisle from hers. They were putting restraints on someone. She couldn't see who it was. If she had to guess, it was either the cell belonging to Devin or Dante. That was if they had even detained him in the same holding area.

"Stick your hands out through the hole," the officer said.

She felt the cold metal of the restraints touch her wrists. It only took a second for the officer to fully restrain her and then he opened the cell door. "Move along," he said, taking her by the arm.

His grip was hard and dug into the back part of her arm, making it hurt. She started to complain but stopped the moment she heard Dante's voice from behind her.

"Get him to the ground," the officer was saying from behind her. She couldn't help but to look back even as the officer escorting her dug even deeper into her arm.

Dante was lying flat down on the floor with his hands restrained behind his back and both officers' knees digging into him. He was screaming profanities until one of the officers smashed a fist into the side of Dante's head.

"Move it," the officer next to her said, tugging her so forcefully, she almost lost her footing and tumbled over. "You don't want to die here, do you?"

She shook her head no.

"We're abandoning ship, so if you want to live then keep up."

Had the ship already taken that much damage? They were near the door leading out of the cell block when the door and a section of the floor vanished in front of her. A large white orb of energy passed through, blinding her, and she fell over backwards. She thought she had heard a scream, but it wasn't until her eyesight returned that she saw what had happened. The young officer that had been escorting her had fallen through the section of flooring missing.

On her hands and knees, she peered over the edge. The lighting was bad, but she could make out the outline of a man laying several decks below. What kind of weapon could do that?

From behind her, coughing and gagging drew her attention. Another section of the room was gone. Either a second orb had passed through or it had been the same orb changing directions. Crumpled on the floor was the lower part of one of the officers she had glimpsed earlier restraining Dante. The upper half of his body was nowhere to be seen, and there wasn't any blood, just a stump of a torso collapsed on the metal flooring.

Behind the stump was the source of the gagging noise. Somehow Dante had managed to free himself from the other officer and his face was buried in the man's throat. Blood was streaming down Dante's face; the officer was trying to fend him off but one of the man's arms was partially gone. It was obvious Dante had locked his jaws into the man and he wasn't letting go. After the officer gave out a final exhale, Dante let the body slump onto the floor in a pool of blood. There was wildness in his eyes as he stared at her.

"What in the hell's happening?" Devin said. His voice came from a cell with the upper level gone, next to Dante.

"Devin, help me," Michelle said, getting to one knee, intending to run.

Dante rolled onto his back and was struggling to slip the restraints from behind him. He had halfway succeeded when her brain finally registered it was time to run. The hole in the floor wasn't large and it was easy to jump over. The door that had been there before was gone and she had open space to run in the semidarkness.

If she could find someone, or even a weapon of some kind .... All thoughts fled from her mind as she was impacted from behind. She went face-down into the flooring which blacked her out for a second. When she came to, she felt someone pressing down on top of her. There was a cooper taste in her mouth, which she wanted to spit out, but she only half succeeded as the person on her back grabbed her hair and pulled hard, lifting her head up off the floor.

She knew who it was long before she heard Dante whisper into her good ear, "It's time to die."

The battle with the ambassador was not going well, Colbosh thought as the ambassador sidestepped another of his attacks. Suntol had attacked at the same time from the opposite side with a fury of his ax cutting through the air. The ambassador managed to trap Suntol's weapon arm with his eyes still closed, and spun him with enough force that Suntol went hurling through the air and crashing into one of the large stone pillars.

Suntol laid face-down on the ground, blood dripping from his mouth and nostrils as he stirred to his feet. His hand that had been holding the ax was limp and looked broken. The ax lay at the ambassador's feet.

Colbosh forced another assault on the ambassador with a fury. No thought to his attack, just primal instinct and rage pouring through his veins and muscles. Like Suntol, the ambassador snatched his blade from his hand with a quickness that was unnatural, and knocked him backwards toward the floor while simultaneously throwing his blade directly at Suntol.

Suntol had just gotten to his feet and was preparing to attack again when the blade struck him deep into the chest. Colbosh couldn't see the reaction on his face because of his impact with the floor. His shoulder took most of the impact and he felt something snap in it, but there was no pain, only rage.

Forcing himself to his feet, he found Suntol had already collapsed to the floor on his knees, looking at the blade planted deep into his chest. Suntol's mouth hung open and then he fell to his side with his chest heaving in and out.

Suntol was gone. The wound he suffered was fatal, Colbosh thought. It was just him now. The ambassador was looking at him now with his eyes wide open, but instead of pupils, there were licking flames of white light pouring from the open slits.

Howling out a final cry for his ancestors to grant him the justice they deserved, Colbosh charged the ambassador again. His body missed as the ambassador stepped away, but Colbosh came back swinging his fist as hard and as fast as was possible for him. All of it was too slow. The ambassador slammed him in the chest with a palm that drove his breath away and shoved him into the pillar next to Suntol's remains.

His brain must have been jarred from the impact because it took his eyes several seconds to focus again. The ambassador had bent over and picked up Suntol's ax from the floor and was moving toward him. Forcing himself to his feet, Colbosh prepared to defend himself.

The ambassador's first attack with the ax smashed into his ribs, burying deep into them. He had not been able to block it, much less escape from the onslaught. The ambassador yanked it free, and on the next strike the edge buried deeply into his forearm. Tendons and muscles were cut and he felt the loss of control of his arm. The injury to his side had to have ruptured some organs. He was feeling numb now and his vision was beginning to fade in and out.

The ambassador's third attack with the ax struck him deep in the stomach, penetrating the human armor he had been wearing. He bent over and collapsed to the floor. If the ax was to be removed this time, then he was sure his bowls would come out with it. The battle was over, he had lost.

Frost and his remaining bridge crew were navigating through the ruined bowels of the *Dawson,* trying to reach an escape pod, when they had heard a struggle nearby.

It didn't take long for some of his seasoned officers to subdue his brother Dante from the prisoner Michelle. One of his men had gotten bit by Dante during the struggle to restrain him, but with a couple of punches to the head Dante was silent at last.

"Are you okay?" Frost asked Michelle as some of the other bridge crew helped her to her feet.

Blood was all over her face and it looked as if she had knocked out a tooth. "Fine," she said. "Devin is still trapped in his cell."

Devin was a prisoner and his safety was nowhere near as important as Frost's crew getting off this ship, but it would make a bad impression on his men if he didn't try to rescue the stranded prisoner.

"The four of you take Dante to the escape pod. Helmsman, come with me." The young man who had been piloting the ship looked nervously at him. His face was pale white.

Michelle led him to the cell with no problem and Frost and the helmsman found the keys on the dead officers.   Devin was glad to be freed and hugged Michelle tight.

"We don't have much time," Frost said.

"What's happening?" Devin said.

"The escape pod is on the next level down. Come on, keep up." he said, running.

They made it to an access ladder and dropped down to the next level. It was as dark as the one above, but Frost and the helmsman both had lights and led the way without trouble. When they arrived at the escape pod a few feet in front of them, was, a wraith blocking the corridor like a sentinel. There was no sign of the others he had sent on ahead, and he could only assume that they were all dead.

"Back away, back away," he said, looking for alternate routes, but there were none.

Before they got too far away from the escape pod, however, the wraith just floated away, like it had no mind of its own. He didn't know what had just happened or what it meant, but damn, he was glad random fortune had smiled on him.

They rushed toward the escape pod. There was no more sign of the wraith; it had just gone. He allowed the others to rush in and he remained by the door, making sure they all got in before he did. He hoped that some of the other bridge crew was still alive, but that wasn't the case. Taking hold of the escape pod door he prepared to enter when something wrapped around his throat from behind.

He struggled at the thing around his throat and found himself stumbling into the escape pod. The others were reacting, but they weren't coming fast; something was holding them back.

"I've always hated you, brother," Dante said as the chains dug even deeper into his throat. Why weren't the others doing something?

To Frost's right he caught a glimpse of something, something bright and glowing. The wraith had returned.

The ambassador's footfalls thundered in his ears. All conscious thoughts were begging to fade from his mind. There was no pain, just icy numbness. The smell of death was in the room. It was the same as it had been on every battlefield he had encountered: that strange, earthy aroma. Through the transparent windows way above him in the chamber, he could see a large fireball streaking through the gray skies. It was a beautiful sight, perhaps even a sign from his ancestors as his last moment passed. But the killing blow never came.

The ambassador was staggering behind him with his hands pressed tightly to his head and his eyes closed. A moment of weakness! His ancestors had answered his prays. With all the strength he had left, he rose to his feet and pulled the blade from his stomach, which lit his body on fire, especially as part of his intestines came out with the edge. With each step his strength grew as he neared the ambassador, who appeared not to know he was approaching.

With slash after slash, he cut down his foe and at last severed his head from the body. He let out a triumphant roar and collapsed to the ground next to his slain enemy. Glory was his. His people could rest now, as could he, and he closed his eyes.

White light leaked from the ambassador's body in white wispy smoke and covered Colbosh's body in a haze. In the back of his mind he became aware of the ships in orbit above; he could feel the life forms that inhabited each of those vessels. There was pain in his body again, but there was also strength returning.

What was happening to him? Strange alien voices filled his ears, but he couldn't understand them.

Michelle watched in horror as Frost was grabbed from behind by Dante. She had unbuckled herself to help, but by the time she drew near them the wraith had appeared again, floating directly in the doorway behind the struggling men. What could she do? If the wraith entered the escape pod, they were all dead.

"Michelle, what are you doing?" Devin said.

She was reacting; she knew what had to be done. Frost and Dante were both standing and they were extremely close to the door. She had to get around them to reach the escape pod release, but she wasn't going around them. She charged into them, pushing with all her might as the men went over backwards and into the waiting embrace of the wraith waiting in the corridor. Both men were consumed instantly. The impact had made her stumble into the door, but she was close enough to the panel that she hit the button that jettisoned the pod from the ship.

"What have you done?" the helmsman said after the escape pod slowed in acceleration. "What have you done?"

"She just saved our lives," Devin said, helping Michelle to a seat.

Outside the tiny windows of the escape pod she could see the remains of the *Dawson*, which was just a dead hulk in space now. Below on the planet there was a thunderous storm brewing, and a large dust cloud in one area, as if something large had impacted the surface of the planet.

"Are you okay?" Devin said.

She grabbed hold of him with both arms and brought him close to her body. For the first time in the last couple of days, she felt fine.

Colbosh got to his feet; it felt strange, as if he were a stranger in his own body. Images of places and things flooded through his mind, places of such beauty and horror that he couldn't even put names to them. His mind couldn't comprehend all of it, but the one thing he did know was the power he had. He had directed his thoughts to the warships above him in space, and the wraiths went to work annihilating all life; to be more efficient, he focused on the power cores of the ships. Several burst after the first onslaught. No empire would be able to stand against him. His ancestors had spared his life in order to bring justice for all the misdeeds done to them. He would use these things to bring that desire to fruition.

As more ships exploded in his mind's eye, something familiar echoed in his mind: voices, not the strange alien ones, but the voices of his own kind. Letting his attention divert, he focused on the voices and discovered places where others of his kind had fled.

His people were all over the galaxy; thousands, if not millions of his people still lived amongst the stars.

Thoughts began to appear in his mind. With this power, he could find and unite all of his people. No empire would dare oppose them, and they could live without fear in this galaxy. Perhaps that was why his ancestors had spared him.